"You must be the most conceited man I've ever met."

Aura coated every syllable with contempt. "What the hell makes you think that I'd choose you over Paul? What really concerns you? The loss of Paul's friendship?"

Flint's smile turned predatory. "Aura, if you understand the concept of friendship at all, you should be able to accept that I'd do almost anything in my power to keep him from the clutches of a greedy little tramp who's been brought up to use her sexy body and beautiful face as a commodity."

ROBYN DONALD has always lived in Northland in New Zealand, initially on her father's stud dairy farm at Warkworth, then in the Bay of Islands, an area of great natural beauty where she lives today with her husband and one corgi dog. She resigned from her teaching position when she found she enjoyed writing romances more, and now spends any time not writing doing reading, gardening, traveling and writing letters to keep up with her two adult children and her friends.

Books by Robyn Donald

HARLEQUIN PRESENTS
1639—PAGAN SURRENDER
1666—PARADISE LOST
1699—ISLAND ENCHANTMENT
1714—THE COLOUR OF MIDNIGHT

ROBYN DONALD

Dark Fire

Harlequin Books

TORONTO • NEW YORK • LONDON
AMSTERDAM • PARIS • SYDNEY • HAMBURG
STOCKHOLM • ATHENS • TOKYO • MILAN
MADRID • WARSAW • BUDAPEST • AUCKLAND

ISBN 0-373-11735-3

DARK FIRE

CHAPTER ONE

WHEN Paul came to pick her up, Aura Forsythe's heart swelled with pride.

He looked so good, the black and white of his evening clothes setting off his fair hair and skin. But she didn't love him for his blond handsomeness. Aura knew, none better, that good looks and regular features had little to do with the person beneath the fleshy veneer.

It had been his smile that first caught her attention, and his air of calm, confident good humour. However, very soon after meeting Paul McAlpine she had realised that he was utterly, completely reliable. It made him irresistible. Over the past three months she'd come to understand him very well, this man she was to marry in a fortnight's time. Bathed in the warmth of his love, her turbulent search for some measure of peace in her life was transformed into serenity. She had never been so happy.

'We're meeting Flint at the restaurant,' he said as he opened the door of his expensive car for her. 'He wants to shower and change, but he'll probably be at Quaglino's before we are.' Flint Jansen was to be best man at their wedding in two weeks' time.

'Where does he live?'

'In Remuera, but he's staying with me.'

'Oh. Why?'

'His place is being redecorated. Wet paint everywhere, so he's going to stay with me for at least a week, and possibly until the wedding.'

He lifted her hand to kiss the slender fingers. Aura's full mouth curved into a smile.

5

'You look very pretty tonight,' Paul murmured as he released her.

'Thank you. I like this dress.'

Although compliments still made her uneasy, experience had trained her to handle them with poise. And compliments from Paul were no threat.

The dress was one she had had for some years, but the rich, muted green silk played up hair the colour of good burgundy wine and ivory skin, darkened and emphasised her huge green eyes.

'So the fabled Flint Jansen is here. It seems odd that I haven't met your best friend yet,' she said, deliberately steadying her voice as she changed the subject with automatic skill.

Paul laughed softly. 'He was saying the same thing. I told him that if he insists on staying in Indonesia for months at a time he must expect things to happen while he's gone.'

Suddenly a car roared across the intersection in front of them. Paul reacted swiftly and without alarm, but Aura was flung forward on to the seatbelt.

'Are you all right?' he asked sharply.

She flashed him a reassuring smile. The way he looked after her, as though she were a precious piece of porcelain, made her feel safe and cherished.

'Yes, I'm fine. You've got very fast reactions.'

His mouth turned up at the corner. 'Not so fast as Flint's. He's like greased lightning. We went hunting in the Uraweras once and he stopped me from going over a cliff.' He paused, then finished enviously, 'Man, did he move! Faster than a king cobra and stronger than a horse. I'm no lightweight, but he hauled me back out of the air as though I were made of balsa wood.'

'He sounds very macho.' Her voice was cool and non-committal.

Paul laughed. 'It's not the way I'd describe him. Macho has a ring of fundamental insecurity to it, whereas

Flint is honest right through. And completely self-sufficient.'

'Honesty,' Aura said cynically, 'can be a much over-rated quality.'

Paul's smile was tender and tolerant. 'Don't try to shock me, darling, I know your little tricks. Although I must admit Flint's complete self-assurance does antagonise people—mostly people who envy it!'

'Well, we all envy the things we haven't got,' Aura agreed, thinking of the many qualities she yearned for.

'How would you know? You've got everything.'

Aura's snort was followed by a smile. 'I'm glad you think so. You and he don't seem to have much in common.'

'We don't, but Flint's the best friend I've ever had. He doesn't suffer fools gladly—if at all—he's about as yielding as granite bedrock, and he has the sort of ominous patience that makes a cat hunting a mouse look testy. But I like him, and I think you will too. He'll certainly be impressed by you. He has an eye for a beautiful woman.'

I'll just bet he has, Aura thought wearily. A cold foreboding sandpapered her nerves. She didn't want to meet Flint Jansen; she already knew she wasn't going to like him.

'He hasn't had much sleep these last few days,' Paul went on. 'He's been tidying up a very hush-hush situation in Indonesia and he strode off the plane looking like something piratical and fierce from the South China Sea.'

'He must be exhausted! Perhaps we should have skipped tonight, and just met at the party tomorrow night.'

'He's tough enough to cope.' Paul smiled indulgently. 'It's inborn. I remember when he first arrived in primary school he was given a rugged time—kids can be little heathens, can't they?—and we've been friends ever since.'

Aura already knew that Flint Jansen and Paul had gone to the same expensive boarding school. She was surprised to hear the rest, however. From the few allusions that Paul had made to his best friend, she'd visualised him as being born able to deal with anything the world threw at him, an iron baby who'd progressed inexorably into an iron child, then hardened more as he grew into an iron man.

'Why did he have such a bad time at school?'

Paul's shoulders lifted. 'Family scandal. His father decamped with a vast amount of other people's money— turned out he'd been spending it on a rather notorious woman who was his mistress. There was a luridly salacious fuss in the newspapers, ending in a court case and even more gaudy revelations. Some of the people his father had defrauded had kids at school. The whole thing got out of hand a bit. Mind you, Flint gave as good as he got, but it was an unhappy couple of years for him.'

'How old was he?'

'Only eight. Old enough to know what was going on, too young to be able to protect himself from older boys who tormented him. Although he tried.' He laughed reminiscently. 'Lord, he must have fought every kid in the school who even looked sideways at him. He didn't care what size they were, and a fair few of them he beat, too.'

Only too well Aura knew what it was like to find no haven from a tormenter. Unwillingly, a pang of fellow feeling softened her attitude. She, too, had been eight when her father had deserted his wife and child to go as a missionary doctor to Africa. Even now, fifteen years later, she felt a shadow of that old grief and bewilderment.

Sighing silently, she told herself that a friend of Paul's had to have a gentler side. At least she and Flint would

have something in common: their mutual affection for
the man who was to be her husband.

But her first sight of the formidable Flint Jansen
changed her mind completely. There was not a hint of
softness in him. At least three inches taller than Paul,
he had to be six foot four, and, with a thin scar curling
in a sinister fashion from his left cheekbone to the arrogant jut of his jaw, his image seared into her brain,
leaving a dark, indelible imprint.

A discord of emotions jostled her, confusing her into
silence; only gradually did she realise that the most pre-
dominant was a turbulent, piercing recognition.

Which was ridiculous, because she had never seen this
man before, not even in a grainy photograph in a newspaper. If she had, she'd have known him; he was not a
man easily forgotten. Beneath the black material of his
dinner jacket his shoulders were broad and powerful. A
crisp white shirt contrasted with skin the bronze of an
ancient artefact. Those wide shoulders and long, heavily
muscled legs beneath smoothly tailored trousers com-
bined with a lithe grace of movement to make him instantly, lethally impressive.

Dark brown hair, conventionally cut, waved sleekly
beneath lights that spun a dangerous red halo around
his head. He had a starkly featured buccaneer's face,
hard and unhandsome, yet it was Flint everyone was
watching from beneath their lashes, not her good-looking
Paul.

The man was awesomely conspicuous, the power of
his personality underlined by a barely curbed, impatient
energy that crackled like lightning across the richly fur-
nished room.

Whatever he might have been like at the age of eight,
Aura thought dazedly as Paul, beaming and endearingly
pompous with pride, introduced them, Flint Jansen certainly didn't need sympathy now; he was more than
capable of dealing with anything life threw at him.

Except that this man didn't deal with anything; he conquered. Flint Jansen made his own terms, and forced the world to accept them.

Smiling stiffly, Aura extended her hand, felt it enveloped by long, strong fingers. It took an effort of will to persuade her unwilling lashes up, and when she did her gaze was captured by golden eyes as clear and startling as a tiger's, with a predator's uncompromising assumption of power and authority, eyes fixed on her face in a gaze that stripped away the superficial mask of her beauty to spotlight the woman who hid behind it. A premonition ran with swift, icy steps through her body and mind.

'Aura,' Flint said in a deep, subtly raw voice that played across her nerve ends with sensual precision. 'Paul's told me several times that you are beautiful, but I thought it was just the maunderings of a man in love. Now I know he understated the case.'

Long past the age when praise for her beauty gave her more than a mild pleasure, Aura winced under a stab of stupid disappointment.

It seemed, she thought ironically, that in spite of that unrestrained magnetism, the fierce, lawless penetration of his glance, Flint Jansen was no more perceptive than other men. The physical accident of her features, the legacy of her ancestors, fooled him as it did most others into believing that her beauty was all she was.

Hoping her maverick chagrin didn't show, she smiled. 'Thank you,' she said aloofly.

His hand was firm and warm and hard, and for a moment the conventional grip felt like some kind of claim, a staking of ownership, a challenge. It took all her self-command not to flinch and pull away.

And then it was over. Their hands relaxed, dropped; Flint turned with a comment that made Paul laugh, and Aura was left wondering whether the shivers that tightened her skin were simply attributable to a cold winter's night and the fact that she, with typical vanity, was wearing no more than the barest essentials beneath her green silk dress.

Of course they were.

Yet as they walked towards the table she felt Flint's probing regard, and once again that eerie sense of dislocation cut her adrift from her usual composure.

Casting a quick upward glance at Paul's pleasant, handsome face, she wondered what on earth her kind, reliable, trustworthy fiancé had in common with this arrogant, intolerant man; it must be one of the mysterious masculine friendships that women couldn't fathom.

Apart from their schooldays, the only attributes they seemed to share were intelligence and ambition. Perhaps they were enough to sustain a friendship.

Paul was rapidly heading for the top of his profession, and people spoke of Flint Jansen as being right in line for position as the next chief executive officer of Robertson's, the big conglomerate he worked for. Paul, a partner in a big City law office, knew a lot about the City, and had told her that the present CEO trusted him implicitly.

Aura understood why. Her first look had convinced her that Flint possessed enough concentrated, effortless authority to take over any organisation, even one as big as Robertson's, and run it with the decision and uncompromising strength that such an enterprise needed.

By the time they arrived at their table tension was jagging through her, snarling up her thought processes, pulling her skin taut. She retained enough presence of mind to smile at various acquaintances, but her whole attention was focused on the man who walked behind her. Although she couldn't see him, she knew when he nodded a couple of times at people who greeted him with transparent interest.

Smiling her thanks at the waiter, Aura allowed him to seat her. As the two men sat down, the little buzz of conversation that had greeted their progress across the room died back to the normal low hum.

Aura drew in a deep breath, purposefully commanding her thudding pulses to slow down, using her considerable willpower to control her wildly unsuitable reactions. Unfortunately, she wasn't given much time to re-erect the barriers of her self-possession.

The formalities of ordering their meals barely over, Flint asked her with a smile that didn't reach his eyes, 'What do you do, Aura? For a living, I mean?'

Talk about throwing down the gauntlet! Clearly, like most of Paul's friends, like his mother, Flint believed that Aura looked at the man she was going to marry with greed rather than love in her heart.

For a fleeting second she wished she had a high-powered, important job to throw in his teeth.

But she hadn't, and it was no use playing for sympathy. Flint Jansen was too hard, too dynamic, too much master of his own destiny to understand the clinging bonds that entangled her.

It wasn't her fault she had no job. In spite of opposition and ridicule she had worked damned hard for her double degree, and if circumstances had been kinder she would already be on the first rungs of her chosen career. Nevertheless, Flint's expression revealed that she wouldn't get anywhere by pleading for understanding.

So with nothing but limpid innocence in her face and voice she looked directly into eyes as clear and sharp as golden crystals, and said, 'Nothing.'

He lifted uncompromising black brows. 'Not a career woman, then.'

There was no scorn in his words, nothing more apparent than mild interest, but the invisible hairs on Aura's skin were pulled upright by a sudden tension.

Cheerfully, yet with a hint of warning in his tone, Paul interposed, 'I know dynamic, forceful, professional women are your cup of tea, Flint, but Aura was brought up the old-fashioned way, so don't you get that note in your voice when you're talking to her. Until the end of last year she was at university. Unfortunately, she also has—responsibilities.'

He and Aura exchanged a glance. Paul not only understood her situation with her mother, he approved of her handling of it.

'Resposibilities?' Flint was smiling, but thick, straight lashes covered the tiger eyes so that it was impossible to see what emotions hid behind that rugged façade.

'A mother,' Aura said lightly, 'and if you think I've been brought up the old-fashioned way, wait till you meet Natalie. She's straight out of the ark.' She primmed her mouth. 'She had a very sheltered upbringing. Her father believed that women were constitutionally incapable of understanding matters more complicated than the set of a sleeve, so he didn't bother to have her taught anything beyond womanly accomplishments like playing the piano and running a dinner party with flair and poise. Consequently she's as sweetly unconcerned about practicalities as a babe in arms.'

'It sounds a considerable responsibility,' Flint agreed in his slightly grating voice. 'Will she be living with you after you—after the wedding?'

At the look of sheer horror that spread over Paul's face, Aura bubbled into laughter. 'No,' she said demurely.

Recovering his equanimity, Paul told him, 'She'll be living quite close to us, so we'll be able to keep an eye on her.'

'I see.' Flint sounded remote and more than a little bored.

Aura asked, 'What are you doing in Indonesia, Mr Jansen?'

'Flint,' he said, smiling with an assured, disturbing magnetism that made every other man in the big, luxurious room fade into the wallpaper. 'I was tidying up a mess.'

'Oh?'

'Don't ask,' Paul advised kindly, directing a purely masculine look at the man opposite. 'He won't tell you anyway. Flint's work is highly confidential.'

Thoroughly irritated by the unspoken male conspiracy, Aura fluttered her lashes and cooed, 'How fascinating. Is it dangerous, too?'

'Sometimes,' Flint said, the intriguing, gravelly texture in his voice intensifying. 'Does danger excite you, Aura?'

From beneath half-closed eyelids he was watching the way the light shimmered across her hair. Uneasily she shook her head; an unknown sensation stirred in the pit of her stomach. Perhaps, instead of letting her hair float around her shoudlers in a gleaming burgundy cloud, she should have confined it into a formal pleat.

'No, far from it,' she said, trying to make her tone easy and inconsequential. 'I'm a complete coward.'

'Aura,' Paul said, touching her hand for a second, 'is not into risk.'

As she turned her head to give him a quick, tender smile, she caught in the corner of her eye the ironic movement of Flint's lips.

'Yet you're getting married,' he said speculatively. 'I've always thought that to be the greatest risk in the world, giving another person such power in your life. Unless, of course, the other person is too besotted to be any threat.'

'Ah, you've guessed my secret,' Paul retorted, his blue eyes warmly caressing as they rested on Aura's face.

Without reason, Aura was hit by a wave of profound disquiet. Her gaze clung a moment to Paul's, then slid sideways as the wine waiter appeared.

When the small business of handing the drinks out was over, Paul began talking of a political scandal that had erupted a couple of weeks before. Hiding an absurd

relief, Aura listened to the deep male voices, sipping her
wine a little faster than usual because something was
keeping her on edge.

No, not something; *someone*, and he was sitting next
to her. If she lowered her eyes she could see Flint's long
fingers on the round tabletop, his bronze skin a shocking
contrast to the white, starched damask cloth. He had a
beautiful hand, lean and masculine and strong.

He had to spend a lot of time in hot sunlight to ac-
quire a tan like that, she thought vaguely. Of course, he
had just returned from the tropics, but, even so, he was
far darker skinned than either her or Paul. It was one
of the reasons those glittering golden eyes were so spectacular, set as they were in black lashes beneath straight
black brows.

The hum of conversation receded, became overlaid by
the sudden throbbing of her heart in her eardrums. From
beneath her lashes Aura's gaze followed his hand as he
lifted his wine glass and sipped some of the pale straw-
coloured liquid. When he'd greeted her the rough
hardness of calluses against her softer palm had made
her catch her breath, and set up a strange, hot melting
at the base of her spine. It had receded somewhat, but
now it was starting all over again.

She didn't know what was happening to her, although
instinct warned her it was dangerous. With a determined
attempt to ignore it, she joined in the conversation.

To share a meal with someone who disapproved profoundly of her was nothing new; hatred she could deal
with.

But Flint Jansen despised her. He had taken one look
at her, and for a frightening second contempt had
flickered like cold flames in the depths of his eyes. The
moment her eyes had focused on that harshly commanding face, an intuition as old as her first female an-
cestor had warned her that he was no friend of hers,

that he never would be. For some reason they were fated to be enemies.

And Paul hadn't noticed.

She looked up at him, half listening as he expounded some interesting point of law to the other man. Apart from her cousin Alick, Paul was the most intelligent man she had ever known, yet he thought they were getting along well.

Flint's textured voice dragged her glance sideways. He was smiling, and even as she tried to jerk her eyes free his gaze snared hers.

For the length of a heartbeat green eyes and gold clashed. His mouth curved in the smiling snarl of a tiger playing with something small and not worthy of it.

A question from Paul shattered the tension, his beloved tones both an intrusion and a shield. As Flint answered, Aura breathed deeply.

Stop it, her brain screamed. But she had no idea what *it* was. Her reaction was totally new to her; it seemed that a new person had moved in to inhabit her body, a bewildering renegade, a woman she didn't know.

She had to calm down, reimpose some sort of control over her wayward responses.

Something Paul said brought a smile to Flint's face, revealing strong white teeth that did more uncomfortable things to the pit of Aura's stomach. Snatching at her slipping self-possession, she concentrated fiercely on the words, not the man; on the occasion, not her reactions.

He had excellent manners. He was entertaining in a dry, wittily cynical fashion. When Aura spoke he listened attentively with nothing more obvious than lazy appreciation in his hooded eyes, yet she felt the track of his eyes like little whips across the clear ivory of her skin. And she sensed his contempt.

Oh, he was clever, he hid it well; he was a man whose feelings were caged by a ferocious will. But Aura had

spent too many years noting hidden, subliminal signals
to be fooled. This was not the casual disdain of a man
faced by a woman out to feather her nest. Flint Jansen's
anger burned with a white-hot intensity that made him
more than dangerous. And all that savage emotion was
directed at her.

It bewildered her and upset her, but the most aston-
ishing thing was that in some obscure way it was exciting. She looked across the table to the shadowed,
clever face slashed by the scar, a countenance almost
primitive in its force and power, and a feral shudder ran
down her spine, set off warning signals all through her,
flashpoints of heat and light leaping from cell to cell.

Shaken, at the mercy of forbidden and equivocal sensations, she managed to disguise her response with a
sparkling glow of laughter and bright conversation, while
Paul watched her with pride and the tiniest hint of possessive smugness. Amazingly, the secret, seething under-
current of ambiguous emotions appeared to swirl around
him without touching him.

She didn't begrudge him his pride; all men, she knew,
wanted to stand well in the eyes of their fellows. It was
at once one of their strengths, and rather endearingly
childish.

'Paul tells me we're having a party tomorrow night,'
Flint said coolly while they waited for dessert.

Natalie had insisted that as mother of the bride she
owed friends and relatives a drinks party. Behind Aura's
back she had wheedled Aura's cousin, Alick Forsythe,
into paying for it, and because she refused to entertain
in the small unit she and Aura lived in now it was being
held at Paul's apartment.

Aura nodded, hoping her irritation didn't show. 'Yes.'
She sent Flint a sideways glance.

His eyes darkened into tawny slits, and for one pulsing
second he watched her as though she'd started to strip

for him. Then his lashes concealed eyes cold and brilliant as the fire in the heart of a diamond.

Aura's mouth dried. 'You'll meet my mother and my bridesmaid, and an assortment of other people. It should be fun.'

'I'm sure it will be.'

Aura resented his bland tone, but more the sardonic quirk of his lips that accompanied it. Although she had fought against the whole idea of this wretched party, now that it was inevitable she was prepared to do what she could to make it a success.

By the time the evening wound towards its close Aura was heartily glad. Every nerve in her body was chafed into painful sensitivity, her head ached dully and bed had never seemed so desirable.

By then she knew she would never like Flint Jansen, and found herself hoping savagely that his job kept him well away from them. The less she saw of the beastly man, the better. Fortunately the feeling was mutual, so she wasn't likely to be plagued with too much of his presence after she and Paul were married.

She expected to be taken straight home, but as Flint held open the car door for her with an aloof, studied smile Paul asked, 'Do you mind if we go back to the apartment first, darling? I'm expecting a call from London, and I'd like to be there when it comes.'

'Yes, of course.'

Halfway there she yawned. Instantly Paul said, 'Poor sweet, you're exhausted, and no wonder. Look, why don't I get off at home, then Flint can drive you the rest of the way? That way you'll be tucked up in bed at a reasonable hour.'

'Oh, no, there's——'

Aura's swift, horrified, thoughtless answer was interrupted by Flint's amused voice from the back seat. 'Sounds like a good idea to me,' he said lazily. 'Where does Aura live?'

Bristling, but recognising that protests would only make her antagonism more obvious, Aura gave him her address.

'Really?'

The hardly hidden speculation in his tone made her prickle. 'Yes,' she said stiffly.

'I know how to get there.'

The hidden insolence in his words scorched her skin with a sudden betraying flush. Aura's tense fingers clasped the beaded work of her fringed Victorian bag. She most emphatically did not want to be cooped up with Flint for the twenty minutes or so it would take to get her home. However, as there was no alternative she was going to have to cope as well as she could.

'Goodnight, sweetheart. Try not to push yourself too hard tomorrow,' Paul said when the transfer of drivers had been effected. He bent down and kissed her gently. 'I'll see you tomorrow night.'

She watched him walk across the footpath and in through the door of the elegant block of apartments where they were going to live until they had children.

Aura bit her lip. She had always thought Paul big, but beside Flint Jansen he was somehow diminished.

With a suddenness that took her by surprise Flint set the car in motion. Aura turned her head to look straight ahead, battered by a ridiculous sense of bereavement, almost of panic.

She searched for some light, innocuous, sophisticated comment. Her mind remained obstinately blank.

The man beside her, driving with skill and control if slightly too much speed, didn't speak either. Aura kept her glance away from his hands on the wheel, but even the thought of them turned her insides to unstable quicksilver. A shattering corollary was the image that flashed into her mind, of those lean tanned hands against the pale translucence of her skin.

Aura stared very hard at the houses on the side of the road. Lights gleamed in windows, on gateposts, highlighted gardens that bore the signs of expensive, skilful attention. Although it was winter, flowers lifted innocent blooms to the shining disc of the moon, early jonquils, daisies, the aristocratic cornucopias of arum lilies. To the left a wall of volcanic stones fenced off a park where the delicate pointed leaves of olive trees moved slightly, their silver reverses shimmering in a swift, soon-dead breeze. Beyond them rose the sharp outlines of a hill.

Aura said sharply, 'This isn't the way.'

'I thought we'd go up One Tree Hill and look at the city lights,' Flint said in his cool, imperturable voice.

Aura's head whipped around. Against the glow of the street-lights his profile was a rigorously autocratic silhouette of high forehead and dominating nose, the clear statement of his mouth, a chin and jaw chiselled into lines of power and force.

Speaking evenly, she said, 'Thanks very much, but I'd rather go straight home.'

A blaze of lights from the showgrounds disclosed his half smile, revealed for a stark moment the narrow, deadly line of the scar. He looked calculating and unreachable. 'That's a pity,' he said calmly. 'I won't keep you long.'

Aura felt the first inchoate stirrings of fear. 'I'm actually rather tired,' she confessed, keeping up the pretence of reluctantly refusing a small treat, trying to smooth a gloss of civilisation over a situation that frightened her needlessly, to hide her uncalled-for alarm and anger with poise and control. 'Organising a wedding is far more exhausting than I'd expected it to be.'

His unamused smile held a distinctly carnivorous gleam.

Oh, lord, she thought frantically, keep things in perspective, Aura, and don't let your imagination run away with you. The man is a barbarian, but he won't hurt you. After all, he's Paul's best friend.

'I'm sure it is,' he said, 'especially at such short notice, but a few minutes spent looking down on the most beautiful city in the world won't hurt you. Who knows, it could even recharge your batteries.'

'It might be dangerous up there,' she said quickly, although she had never heard of anything unpleasant happening on top of One Tree Hill.

His laughter was brief and unamused. 'I don't think so.'

She didn't think so, either. For other people, possibly, but not the ruthlessly competent Flint Jansen.

Opening her mouth to object further, she cast a fulminating glance at that inexorable profile then closed it again. He was a man who made up his mind and didn't let anyone change it.

The exact reverse of her mother, Aura thought acidly, trying to fight back the fear that curled with sinister menace through her. Natalie's mind was like a straw caught in a summer wind, whirled this way and that by each small eddy, held only on one course, that of her own self-interest.

Flint Jansen was bedrock, immovable, dominating, impervious, a threat to any woman's peace of mind. Even a woman in love with another man.

Aura pretended to look about her as they wound up the sides of the terraced volcano and along the narrow ridges. For centuries the Maori settlers of New Zealand had grown kumara in the fertile volcanic soil of the little craters below, but the rows of sweet potato were long gone and now sheep cropped English grasses there.

At the top the car park was empty. Nobody looked down over the spangled carpet of city lights, no one gazed up at the obelisk past the lone pine tree, past the statue of the Maori warrior, past the grave of the pioneer who had given this green oasis to the people of Auckland,

nobody gazed with her into the black infinity that ached
in Aura's heart, the unimaginable reaches of space.

Switching off the engine, Flint turned to look at her.
The consuming heat of his scrutiny seared her skin, yet
banished immediately the haunted isolation, the insig-
nificance she felt whenever she looked at the night sky.

Tension crawled between her shoulder-blades,
tightened every sinew in her body, clogged her breath
and her pulse, made her eyes dilate and her skin creep.
When he spoke she recoiled in nervous shock.

'I assume,' he drawled, 'that you know what you're
doing.'

She ran the tip of her tongue along dry lips. 'I assume
so, too. In what particular thing?'

'Marrying Paul.'

It had to be that, of course. So why did she feel as
though they were talking about two different subjects?
She was letting him get to her. Calmly, and with a confidence that sounded genuine, she said, 'Oh, yes, I know
exactly what I'm doing.'

'I do hope so, pretty lady. For everyone's sake. Because
if you do to him what you've done to two others and
jilt him, you're in trouble. Paul may be too besotted to
deal with you properly, but I'm not.'

For a moment Aura couldn't speak. Then she returned haughtily, 'I presume you've been snooping
through my life.'

'Yes.' He sounded as though her naïveté amused him.

Aura felt sick, but she managed to keep her voice
steady, almost objective. 'Mr Jansen——'

His smile was cold and mirthless. 'You've been calling
me Flint all evening. Reverting to my surname now is
not going to put any distance between us.'

She said aridly, 'Flint then. I won't hurt Paul in any
way, if that's what you're afraid of. I'm going to make
him very happy. This time it's real.'

'I suppose each of the other poor fools you were engaged to thought it was real, too.' He paused, and when she didn't reply, added, 'And presumably that you'd make them very happy.'

The obvious sexual innuendo made her feel sick. She stared sightlessly ahead. 'Paul knows about them,' she said.

'So it's none of my business?'

'Exactly.'

'Not even when he finds out—as he's bound to do— that you're not in love with him?'

Aura said angrily, 'I love him very much.'

He laughed softly, an immense cynicism colouring his tone. 'Oh, I have to admire the languishing glances, the smiles and the gentle touches. But they didn't look like love to me, and if Paul wasn't so enamoured that he can't think straight he'd know that what you feel for him is not the sort of love that leads to a happy marriage.'

'You'd know all about it, I suppose.' Struggling for control, she caught her breath. 'I love him,' she repeated at last, but the conviction in her voice was eaten away by a sense of futility. One quick glance at Flint's unyielding profile and she knew that whatever she said, she couldn't convince this man.

'Just as you'd love your older brother, with respect and admiration and even a bit of gratitude,' he agreed dispassionately. 'But that's not what marrige is all about, beautiful, seductive, sexy Aura. It's also about lying in a bed with him, making love, giving yourself to him, accepting his body, his sexuality with complete trust and enthusiasm.'

Her small gasp echoed in the darkened car. She searched for some reply, but her mind was held prisoner by the bleak and studied impersonality of his tone.

After a moment he continued, 'When Paul looks at you it's with love, but I don't see much more in you than satisfaction at having got what you want: a complacent and easygoing husband.'

Stonily, Aura said, 'I want to go home.'

'I'm sure you do.' He sounded amused, almost lazily so, and satisfied, as though her reaction was just what he had expected. 'But you're going to stay here until I've finished.'

'What gives you the right to talk like this to me?'

The words tumbled out, hot with feeling, shamingly defiant, giving away far more than was wise. Aura tried desperately to curb the wild temper that used to get her into so much trouble before she found ways to restrain it.

'Paul is my friend,' Flint said coolly. 'I care about him and his happiness. And I'd hate to see him tied to a calculating little tramp when a few words could save him. That's what friends are for, surely?' The last question was drawled with mockery.

She didn't intend to hit him. In fact, she didn't even realise she had until the high sweep of his cheekbone stopped her hand with such implacable suddenness that every bone in her arm ached with the impact.

Gulping with shock and pain, she snatched her hand back, cradled it to her stomach and said in a voice she had hoped never to hear again, 'Don't you call me a tramp. Don't *ever* call me a tramp.'

He hadn't moved. For long, taut seconds the imprint of her hand, white in the darkness, stood out with stark, disgraceful precision.

So coldly that it congealed even her righteous indignation, he said, 'Why not? You're selling yourself to him. That's what tramps do. Money for sexual services.'

'I am *not* selling myself to him.' Her voice cracked, but she rushed on, hurling the words at him, 'And it's not just sex, damn you, you ignorant swine, there's more——'

'Not much more. For you it's security, for him love. You need his money, he wants to spend the rest of your life making you happy. And, not so incidentally, sleeping with you. If that's the bargain it's fair enough, I suppose. Just don't renege on it, Aura, when he's so far under your spell that the poor sod can't crawl out.'

It took a vast effort to moderate her tone, to summon the cadences of bored sophistication, but Aura hoped she managed it. 'Paul is thirty-two—old enough, don't you think, to fall in love without needing someone to vet his choice?'

'Paul is a romantic,' he returned unemotionally. 'And God knows, you're enough to turn even the most level-headed man's brain into mush. However, I'm not in the least romantic. I've seen enough women who looked like angels and behaved like the scourings of the streets to be able to ignore huge green eyes scattered with gold dust and a mouth that's full and sulkily cushioned with promises of unattainable erotic delights. Even so, I took one look at you and found myself wondering.'

'Wondering what?' The moment the words trembled from her lips she knew she'd made a mistake. 'It doesn't m——'

But he interrupted with blasé precision. 'Wondering whether in bed you live up to the promises you make.'

Aura froze as nausea climbed her throat. Sexy talk, the kind of sensual, seductive words that men used when they wanted to coax a woman into bed, made her shiver with an unremitting fear.

She had been barely fourteen when the husband of one of her mother's friends had told her of his fantasies, all of them starring her, as he drove her home from the house where he lived with his wife and three children. He had seemed to think that her beauty gave him the right to tell her specifically just what he wanted to do to her, in bed and out. His words had been detailed and obscene, summoning scenarios that chilled her right through to her soul.

He had made no attempt to touch her, then or ever, but his perverted pleasure in seeing the shock and fear in her face had destroyed her innocence.

Sickened and disgusted, she had spent the next three years avoiding him, until eventually she had found the courage to threaten him with disclosure of his sexual harassment.

Since then other men had accused her of teasing, of being provocative, believing that her face was the mirror of her character, that the intensity of their desire put her under an obligation to respond.

Oh, she had learned to deal with them; she knew when a light touch was needed, when indignation and threats were necessary. But she had been scarred, her inner soul as much mutilated as whatever had slashed through Flint's skin. And she still felt that sick helplessness when a man looked at her with that knowing speculation, when a certain thickness appeared in his voice. She hated being fodder for fantasy.

Strangely enough, in spite of Flint's words, she didn't feel that sinking nausea now.

One of the things she liked so much about Paul was his light touch, his wry, self-deprecating amusement. He never made her feel that he wanted too much from her, and when he looked at her it was without greed, with tenderness. She felt safe with Paul.

Since that first experience she had viewed compliments on her looks as preliminaries to demands she had no intention of satisyfing, but listening to Flint Jansen's gravelly voice as he passionlessly catalogued her physical assets brought heat bursting through her in a drenching flood of sensation.

Appalled, mortified, she said huskily, 'Mr—Flint, I know you're Paul's oldest friend, and I know you and he are very fond of each other, but you shouldn't be talking to me like this. I'm going to make Paul very happy. Please take me home.'

'I hope you mean that,' he said, every menacing syllable clear and silky above the pounding of her heart, 'because if you don't, beautiful Aura, if you find a richer man than Paul one day and decide to shuck him off like an old coat, I'll come looking for you. And when I find you, I'll make you sorrier than you've ever thought you could be.'

CHAPTER TWO

WITHOUT waiting for a reply he switched on the engine and backed the car around, then set off down the hill while Aura fought the hardest battle of her life. Never before, not even in childhood when she had been notorious for tantrums, had she been so furiously incandescent with rage, a rage all the more difficult to deal with because it was stretched like a fragile cloak over debilitating fear.

What an arrogant, brutal, cocksure, conceited *bastard*! Oh, she would like to ruin Flint Jansen's life, she'd love to have him come begging to her so she could spurn him with a haughty smile. She'd turn sharply on her heel and walk away, she'd make him *grovel*——

Shaking with frustration and fury, horrified by her thoughts, she dragged air into painful lungs, then set her mind to looking coolly and rationally at the situation.

Eventually, after a huge expenditure of willpower, she succeeded.

In one way Flint's attitude was rather touching. So often the only feelings men allowed themselves to express were connected with anger. Flint's suspicions at least showed he had Paul's interests at heart.

And, viewed objectively, someone who had been engaged twice before had to be a risk in the matrimonial stakes. If you didn't know the circumstances, such a history did seem to show a certain lack of staying power.

Unfortunately, her eminently rational thoughts did nothing to ease the fury that simmered beneath her imposed and artificial restraint. Flint *didn't* know the circumstances; he had just jumped to conclusions, so how dared he accuse her of being a tramp, of not loving Paul, of marrying him for his money?

Nothing would give her greater pleasure than to rub every word in his face, force him to acknowledge that he was wrong...

After another calming breath she tried to convince herself that all she had to do was make Paul happy. If she did that, Flint would be compelled to admit how very wrong he was. Staring blindly through the windscreen, she conjured up a vivid and highly satisfactory scenario of her and Paul's twenty-fifth wedding anniversary, when Flint, proud head lowered, would have to grovel. She could see his face so clearly, see the gracious smile with which she received his abject apology...

Much later, she realised that Paul had not appeared at all in this immensely gratifying dream. The scene that sprang fullblown from the depths of her brain had only two players—her and Flint Jansen.

Neither spoke until they reached the unit. Aura made to open the door, but Flint said crisply as he turned the engine off, 'I'll see you inside.'

'You don't need to,' she said, curt words spilling into the cold silence like little pebbles thrown into sand.

Taking no notice, he got out and came around the front of the car. For those moments, as the street-lights edged his silhouette in gold, he looked like some dark huntsman straight out of myth, lean and lithe and supernaturally big, an ominous, threatening, purposeful presence in the quiet, seedy suburban street.

Holding herself rigidly aloof, Aura slid her long legs out of the car and stood up, then preceded him down the path. A light inside revealed that her mother hadn't gone to bed.

The last thing Aura wanted just then was for them to meet. Her emotions were too raw and antagonistic to be properly controlled, so at the door she turned and said with what she hoped was aplomb, 'Thank you for the ride home. Goodnight.'

Unfortunately, before he had a chance to answer, the door opened.

'Paul,' Natalie cooed in the voice she reserved for him alone, 'dear boy, *do* come in! I want to talk to you about the new flat—I was thinking that what it really needs is a new——'

'Paul didn't bring me home,' Aura interrupted swiftly.

Her mother peered past her, her eyes widening. 'Neither he did,' she said.

Aura watched her regroup as she surveyed Flint. Over her mother's face flashed the famous smile that had reduced so many men to abject submission.

'Darling,' she purred languidly, 'don't just stand there letting me make a fool of myself, introduce us.'

With angry resignation Aura complied, heard her mother invite Flint inside, and his immediate acceptance. It was useless glaring at Natalie, who was invulnerable to suggestion, but Aura sent a contemptuous glance at the man smiling with cynically amused admiration down at her mother.

As though it impacted physically on him he lifted his head, returning Aura's fulminating glower with a long, considering look from narrowed eyes that challenged her to object.

To her fury and despair, Aura couldn't meet his gaze. Turning away, she dumped her bag on the table with a short, abrupt movement.

'How kind of you to bring Aura home, Flint. You must have a nightcap before you go,' Natalie said sweetly, making expert play with her lashes as she ushered him into the cluttered little sitting-room. 'Whisky, surely? You look like a whisky man. I think we've got some somewhere.'

His expression reminded Aura of the smile on the face of the tiger. 'Not for me, thank you.'

Aura bit her lip. She should have been pleased at this unusual interest. Following Lionel's death and the subsequent revelations of his shady, secret life, her mother had sunk into a dangerous apathy that developed into a fullblown nervous breakdown when she'd realised that the only assets she had left were a small annuity Lionel hadn't been able to get his hands on. It provided barely enough money to keep her.

For the first time in her life, Aura had found herself needed by her mother. At first she hadn't understood how ill Natalie was, but when she'd come home from a much-wanted job interview to find her unconscious from an overdose of sleeping pills and tranquillisers, she had realised that for the time being she was going to have to give up her ambitions to make a career in marketing.

Even then, she had hoped that she would have time to finish designing a market research programme she had begun at university. Unfortunately, Natalie had needed her constant attention, and as the tap of the computer's keys seemed to drive her to a frenzy, Aura had given up on it for the time being.

It had been a miserable six months. The only thing that had sustained Aura was meeting Paul. It had helped Natalie, too. She was slowly returning to her normal spirits.

Witness, Aura thought grimly, her swift reaction to Flint Jansen.

It was difficult to see what was going on behind the clear, hard glitter of Flint's eyes, but Aura was prepared to bet that it was appreciation. The clear skin and sultry green eyes Natalie had bequeathed to her daughter were almost unmarred by the years. Tiny lines of petulance and self-indulgence were beginning to etch into the ivory skin, drag the full, lush mouth down at the corners. Even so, Natalie was exquisitely beautiful.

'No?' she said now, with a knowing, flirtatious smile. 'Well, then, a cup of coffee, and while it's being made you must sit down and tell me how you come to be driving Aura home.'

'Paul had to wait for a phone call from Britain,' Aura interposed curtly, not caring whether he thought her rude, 'so Flint very kindly offered to take his place.'

'Only for the drive back,' Flint said in a voice as smooth and bland as cream.

Flakes of colour heated Aura's cheeks. 'Naturally,' she retorted too quickly.

'I'm staying with Paul until the wedding,' Flint told Natalie, 'so if you want me to take a message to him, I'll do it gladly.'

Aura's brows drew together as she stared significantly at her mother, willing her to be silent. But Natalie had learned that the best way to get what she wanted was to use a mixture of cajolery and sexuality on the most powerful man within sight, and it was too late for her to study new tactics.

'No, no,' she said, smiling at Flint as though he was the most fascinating man she had ever met, 'it's just the new flat. I couldn't work out what I didn't like about it, and only a few minutes ago when I was sitting looking at this hideous affair here I realised that it was the carpet. Too middle class and tacky. We'll have to get it changed, but don't you worry about it, I'll discuss it with Paul when I see him next. Now, do sit down and tell me all about yourself. Aura, aren't you going to make us some coffee, darling?'

Sure that Flint was too astute to be taken in by her mother's calculated seductiveness, she watched with astonishment when he gave her mother a slow, tantalising smile and sat down.

Natalie, who adored flirtations and knew just how to conduct one, eyed his hard, unhandsome face with an interest that had something of avidity in it, and proceeded to show how skilled she was in such sport.

Flint responded to her sophisticated coquettishness with a lazy, dangerous charm that had Natalie eating out of his hand in no time. Fuming, Aura had to make coffee and listen to her mother being questioned by an expert. Within five minutes Natalie had artlessly divulged that dear, kind, *thoughtful* Paul had not only bought a flat for his mother-in-law to be, but had also offered a car.

'Only to have Aura throw it back in his face,' Natalie sighed. 'So middle class and boring and prissy of her! It would make life infinitely less stressful, especially now. As it is, unless friends are generous enough to put themselves out for us, we have to use public transport.'

Her voice registered the kind of horror most people reserved for crawling over oyster shells. Flint's brows shot up.

Much encouraged by this, Natalie went on, 'And what difference is there between moving before the wedding and moving after it? I'm not complaining, but it would have made life so much easier for us all if we'd had the new flat, which is four times the size of this dreary little place, to entertain. But no, Aura had some idea that it wasn't the done thing. As though I'm no judge! Not that it really matters, it just means that I'll be stuck here until they come home from their honeymoon. I've been ill, so I can't cope with moving by myself.'

Whenever it seemed she might run down, Flint asked another seemingly innocuous question, and away she went again, spilling out things Aura would much rather he didn't know. Cosseted and adored all her life, Natalie had been valued only for her looks, for her pleasing ways. She naturally gravitated towards men who looked as though they could protect her. Flint filled the bill perfectly.

If you liked that sort of overt, brash male forcefulness. Aura's fingers trembled as she set the tray. She knew she was being unfair; Flint's air of competence, of authority, that inbuilt assurance that here was a man who was master of himself and his world, was not assumed. It was as natural a part of him as his smile and the complex hints of danger that crackled around him.

Aura knew better than to display her anger and resentment, but when she appeared with the tray she very firmly took command of the conversation, steering it away from personal things to focus on the man who sat opposite, his lean, clever, formidable face hiding every thought but those he wanted them to see.

Fortunately, Natalie knew that men adored talking about themselves. She demanded the details of his life, so they learned that he was some kind of troubleshooter for his firm, that he travelled a lot overseas, that he had been born in the Wairarapa and still went back as often as he could, and that he was thirty-one, a year younger than Paul.

Which, Aura thought as she sipped her coffee, probably explained Paul's protective attitude to him at school. He certainly didn't need protecting now. A more confident, invulnerable man than Flint Jansen it would be hard to imagine. She could see him troubleshooting right across the globe, keen intelligence fortified by disciplined energy and confident control, the hard-edged masculine charisma warning all who came up against him that here was a man who had to be taken very seriously indeed.

He could tell a good story, too. In a very short time he had them both laughing, yet although he seemed perfectly open Aura realised that he was revealing very little of either his work or himself. What they were being treated to was a skilfully edited version of his life, one he'd clearly used before.

A quick, unremarked glance at her watch informed her that he had only been there thirty minutes. It seemed hours. Restlessly, she thought she'd never be able to look around the small, slightly squalid room, rendered even smaller by the furniture that her mother had managed to salvage from the wreck of her life, without remembering Flint in it. Somehow he had managed to stamp the dark fire of his personality on it as Paul never had.

At least he hadn't paid much attention to her; his whole concentration had been almost entirely on her mother.

Which worried Aura. She knew skilful pumping when she heard it, and thanks to Natalie he now knew that they had no money beyond her pathetic little annuity. Natalie even told him all about Alick's generosity over the years, thereby reinforcing, Aura thought savagely, his estimation of both Forsythe women as greedy and out for what they could get.

Still, it didn't really matter. Paul knew she wasn't like that, and Paul's opinion was the only one she cared about.

Perhaps he had noticed that surreptitious glance at her watch, for almost immediately he rose. Aura overrode her mother's protests by telling her crisply that Flint had been flying most of the day and must be exhausted.

'You don't look tired,' Natalie murmured. 'You look— very vigorous.'

Aura stirred uneasily. She was accustomed to her mother's innuendoes, but her coyness grated unbearably.

Flint's smile hid a taunt as he responded, 'Aura's right, I need some sleep.'

'Ah, well, we'll see you tomorrow,' Natalie said sweetly, looking up at him from beneath her lashes. She held out her hand. It was engulfed by his, but instead of shaking it he kissed her pampered fingers with an air.

Natalie laughed and bridled and, amazingly, blushed.

Austerely, Aura said, 'Goodnight.' She did not hold out her hand.

His smile was measured, more than a little cold-blooded. 'I'll be seeing you,' he said, and somehow the words, spoken softly in that sensuously roughened voice, sent shivers down her spine.

When at last he was gone, and Aura was able to breathe again, she said drily, 'Well, there's no need for him to ask any more questions. You've told him all he ever needs to know about us.'

'Oh, for heaven's sake, Aura, try not to be too drearily bourgeois.' Into the weary flatness of her mother's tone there crept a note that could have been spite as she added, 'You're not the tiniest bit jealous because he wasn't interested in you, are you?'

For some obscure reason that hurt. Aura's lips parted on a swift retort, then closed firmly before the hot words had a chance to burst out. Over the years she had learned how to deal with her mother, and an angry response was the worst way. The nasty incident on One Tree Hill must have shaken her usual restraint.

Smiling wryly she said, 'No, not in the least. You can have the dishy Flint; your friends might laugh at the difference in ages, but they'll probably envy you. However, I wouldn't bore him with any more details of our personal affairs, or you'll see him rush off to more exciting conversation.'

From her mother's expression she saw that her shaft had struck home. If Flint Jansen pumped her mother again he'd probably get what he wanted easily enough—he was that sort of man—but with any luck, from now on Natalie wouldn't spill out unasked-for details.

It had been a strange day. As Aura curled up in her cramped room and closed her eyes against the glare of the streetlight that managed to find her face every night through the gap between the blind and the window-frame, she tried to woo sleep with an incantation that never failed.

In two weeks' time she would be married to Paul, darling, gentle, kind, understanding Paul, and she would be able to relax and live the serene, happy life she had always longed for.

Of course there would be troubles, but they'd be able to overcome them together. Her mother, for one. Natalie would always demand the constant attention she considered her due. But when they were married, Aura's first loyalty would be to Paul. Dearest Paul. She intended to make him so happy, as happy as he would make her.

Two weeks. A fortnight. Only fourteen more days.

Firmly banishing Flint Jansen's fiercely chiselled face from her mind, she turned her head and drifted off to sleep.

She woke the next morning slightly headachey and as edgy as a cat whose fur had been stroked the wrong way. The clear sky of the night before had been transmuted into a dank, overhanging pall of heavy cloud; rain hushed persistently against the window panes.

Listening to the early traffic swish by on the road outside, she wondered why she felt as though she had spent all night in a smoky room. It couldn't be the weather. It had rained for most of the autumn, so she was quite reconciled to a wet wedding day.

And everything was under control. Mentally she went through the list. The caterer knew to ignore any instructions her mother gave; her wedding-dress was made in the simple, flowing lines that suited both her figure and the informal occasion, not the elaborate and unsuitable costume Natalie had suggested. And the florist had no illusions about the sort of flowers she wanted.

A wedding, even one as small as theirs, was like a juggernaut, caught up in its own momentum, rolling serenely on towards an inevitable conclusion. The simile made her smile, and stretch languidly. This wedding was going to be perfect, from the hymns to the best man——

Flint Jansen.

Like the outburst of a nova the memory of the previous evening lit up her mind, and with a shame that sickened her she recalled the dream that had woken her halfway through the night. Explicit, sensual, only too vivid, they had lain tangled together in a bed swathed with white netting. Through the wide windows came the soft sounds of the sea. Scents that hinted at the tropics floated on the heated, drowsy air.

She tried to convince herself that the other man in that wide bed had been Paul, but it was Flint's bronzed, harsh-featured face that had been above hers, Flint's hard mouth that had kissed her with such passion and such bold eroticism, Flint who had touched her in ways Paul never had.

'Oh, God,' she whispered, burying her face into her hot pillow.

Somehow Flint Jansen had slid right through her defences and taken over that most unmanageable part of her mind, the hidden area that manufactured dreams and symbols, the secret source of the imagination. Such a betrayal had never happened to her before.

Perhaps that vengeful little daydream on the way home from One Tree Hill had given her inner self permission to fantasise? Had the strength of her anger carried over into her unconscious and been transmuted for some reason into the passion she hadn't yet known?

In the end, after mulling over the whole wretched business for far too long, she was forced to accept that for some reason she was physically attracted to Flint.

Of course it had nothing to do with love, it was a mere matter of chemicals. Aura might be relatively unsophisticated, but she knew that such an explosion of the senses usually died as quickly as it flamed into being. She had seen what happened to those of her friends who believed it to be love. They had found that within a horrifyingly short time, when desire was sated, they were left with nothing but the dross of a failed affair.

Jessica Stratton, her best friend and bridesmaid, had tripped into such a pit only a year ago. Recalling the subsequent disillusionment, Aura sat up, shivering in the cold dampness of her room, and reached for her dressing-gown.

'I don't even *like* him,' Jessica had wailed. 'I thought it was the greatest romance since Romeo and Juliet, I thought he was wonderful, and then I woke up beside him one morning and saw a boorish, sports-mad yob with hairy toes and a bad case of egotism. He wasn't even a good lover; he did it by numbers! What on earth did I see in him?'

'Chemistry,' Aura had told her pertly, secretly rather proud that she had never fallen prey to it.

Clearly pride went before a fall. Because when she looked at Flint Jansen funny things happened to her legs and her spine, and her insides melted into a strangeness that was shot through with exhilaration and eagerness.

Paul's touch was warmth, and love, and happiness. What she felt when Flint looked at her was a heated sexual excitement, the basic lust of a woman for the most potent man around.

Her soft, full mouth firmed in distaste as she shrugged into her robe and tied it. Appetite, that was all it was, a primeval pull at the senses, a straight biological urge that had nothing to do with love or trust. She-animals felt its force, and mated with the strongest male because of it.

In spite of his striking, unhandsome face and un-yielding expression, Flint was a very sexy man, edged with an aura of danger that some women found smoulderingly sensual. However, she was immune to what he offered.

Uncomfortable and disturbing although her reaction to Flint was, she could deal with it. All she had to do was remember that it would pass. She would not ex-change the pure gold of her feeling for Paul, the affection and companionship, the fact that she respected and admired and loved him, for all the enticing tinsel and gloss of sexual desire, however it blazed in the moonlight.

Braced by common sense, Aura showered and cleaned her teeth in the tiny, dingy bathroom, then made coffee and took her mother the glass of mineral water and slice of lemon that was her first meal of the day. When that was done she sat down to her toast in the dining end of the sitting-room.

Almost immediately the telephone rang. 'Hello, sweetheart,' Paul said. 'Everything all right for tonight?'

'So far, so good.' Aura smiled at the gloomy day outside. 'I've no doubt there'll be more crises today, but at the moment I'm on top of everything.'

She could hear his smile. 'Good. How did you get on with Flint last night?'

So unnerved was Aura by her dreams that she immediately wondered whether somehow he knew...

No, of course he couldn't!

'Fine,' she said automatically. 'It was rather touching, really. He took me to the top of One Tree Hill and tried to satisfy himself that I have your best interests at heart.'

There was a moment of silence before Paul said in an amused voice, 'Did he, indeed? And do you think you convinced him? Or did you tell him to mind his own business?'

Aura laughed softly. 'You know me too well. To be honest, I don't really care what he thinks. If I convince you, that's all I worry about. And I've got a long time to do that; at least sixty years.'

With immense tenderness he said, 'Darling, I love you.'

'I love you, too.'

'Not as much as you're going to,' he said quietly, almost as though he was making a vow. Before she could answer he said, 'Enough of this! I can't spend all morning dallying with you, I've got work to do. It's this afternoon you're going to do the flowers, isn't it, so you'll be here when the caterers come at three?'

'Yes. It shouldn't take me more than an hour to arrange the flowers, and all I've got to do for the caterers is show them where things are in the kitchen. I'll have plenty of time to come home and get changed before you pick me up.'

'Good. Although it would take a lot less time if you'd just get off your high horse and accept a car. All right, we've been through it all, but you must be the most stubborn, exasperating woman I've ever met. I have to go, darling, I can hear Flint surfacing, and if I'm not to be late I have to leave within three minutes.'

Aura hung up, wondering whether Flint would be in the flat that afternoon.

Of course not, she scoffed as she finished her toast and drank a cup of coffee. He had this important, slightly sinister-sounding job; he'd be at work giving the women there a thrill.

After the final fitting of the wedding-dress, she had lunch with an old friend of her grandmother's before catching the bus to Paul's apartment, walking the last hundred metres through the downpour that had been threatening all day. Her umbrella saved her head and shoulders, but she grimaced at the cold wetness of the rain on her legs and shoes. Much of this, and she'd have to think of getting a coat.

No, she thought as the last of the autumn leaves fluttered like dank brown parachutes to land in a soggy layer on the footpath, after they were married she'd have a car and life would be more convenient. But she still didn't regret not having accepted Paul's offer.

At least Flint couldn't accuse her of unseemly greed.

Even the perfect, radiant flowers of the camellias were turning brown under the rain's relentless attack, while pink and white and yellow daisies were being beaten into the dirt. In one garden dahlia plants in a wide bed were still green and leafy at the base; only the stalks that had held the brilliant flowers towards the sun were blackened and stiff.

Aura was overcome by a sudden, stringent melancholy, a weariness of the spirit that gripped her heart. It was the weather, she thought, shaking off her umbrella before she tapped out the code that opened the street door of the apartment complex. June was often fine, but this year it had decided to go straight into winter.

In two weeks' time she'd be married to the nicest man she had ever met, and they would be flying to a luxurious little island of the coast of Fiji for their honeymoon, where she would have nothing to do but soak up the heat and the soft tropical ambience, and learn how to please Paul.

As though summoned by an evil angel, Flint's voice echoed mockingly through her mind. 'It's about lying in a bed with him, making love, giving yourself to him, accepting his body, his sexuality with complete trust and enthusiasm . . .'

The door opened to her suddenly unsteady hand. She walked quickly across the foyer, nodding to the porter, her heels tapping coldly on the smooth, shiny marble. In the lift she pressed the button for the third floor.

Oh, she was a fool, letting him get to her like that. Of course she wanted to make love with Paul; she enjoyed his kisses, his caresses, they made her feel warm and loved and secure. That was why she had broken the other two engagements. Although she had liked both men very much, she had been unable to let them touch her beyond the mildest of caresses.

Paul was different. He had understood her wariness, the tentative fear she had never really overcome, and he hadn't tried to rush her into a sexual relationship before they were married.

Of course Flint didn't have the faintest idea that she was still a virgin! Forcing her mind away from his relentless tone as he accused her of being no better than a whore, she opened the door into Paul's apartment.

The flowers had already arrived. Great sheaves of roses and carnations and Peruvian lilies stood in buckets in the kitchen, with sprays of little Singapore orchids and exquisitely bold cymbidiums, all in shades of pink and bronze and creamy-green. After hanging up her coat, Aura tried to banish her odd weariness by walking slowly around the big rooms of the flat, working out where to put vases.

An hour later she was arranging the roses in a huge vase on the hall table when, against the sounds of Kiri Te Kanawa's magnificent voice singing Gershwin, she heard the front door open. A quick glance over her shoulder revealed the lean form of Flint Jansen strolling in through the door, completely at home, a perfectly detestable smile not softening his arrogant face.

Aura's eyes evaded his and flew to the cheek she had slapped. Little sign of the blow remained, except for a slight reddening of the skin about the thin scar. Remorse and self-disgust roiled unpleasantly inside her.

'Hello,' she said, nervously banishing the fragmented images of last night's dream that threatened to surge up from wherever she had marooned them.

The smile widened as he conducted a leisurely survey. Aura had slid her wet shoes off and was standing barefoot in a narrow tan skirt topped by a jersey the exact gold at the heart of the big cream chrysanthemums; her bronze and dark brown scarf was twisted a little sideways. Beneath Flint's narrowed scrutiny she felt like an urchin.

'The spirit of autumm,' he said blandly, closing the door behind him and advancing into the hall. 'Don't let me interrupt you.'

'I won't.' It was a short answer and far too revealing, but she felt as though someone had tilted the stable world on which she stood. An odd breathlessness made it difficult for her to speak. Turning back to the flowers, she pushed a splendid bronze-pink candelabrum of cymbidiums home.

'I'm sorry I slapped you last night,' she said abruptly.

Silence stretched tautly between them. She kept her eyes on the flowers in the vase.

'Are you? I didn't leave you with much option.' There was no measurable emotion in his tone, nothing to tell her what he was thinking.

Her shoulders moved. 'Nevertheless,' she said gruffly, thrusting another large sprig of black matipo into the back of the arrangement, 'I don't normally go around hitting people.'

'Your apology is accepted.' Clearly he didn't care a bit.

From the corner of her eye she watched him pick up one of the long-stemmed rosebuds. Hastily Aura averted her gaze, strangely affected by the sight of the fragile flower held so carefully in his lean strong hand as he raised it to his face.

'It has no scent,' he said on a detached note.

'No. Most flowers cultivated for the markets have lost their scent. Even the carnations have very little.' She was babbling, so she drew in a deep breath. Much more of his presence, she thought with slight hysteria, and she'd end up hyperventilating.

'A pity. I'd rather have scent and fewer inches in the stem.'

'Not all roses have scent.'

'I prefer the ones that do.'

She nodded. 'So do I.'

He held out the stem. Carefully avoiding his fingers, she took it.

'Will they open?' he asked.

She shrugged, and put the rose into the vase. 'I don't know. Sometimes they do, sometimes they die like that.'

'Poor things. No scent, no blossoming, no seeding. Hardly flowers at all. I wonder what gave anyone the idea that these were preferable to the real thing.' He walked into the sitting-room, saying off-handedly, 'I'll get you a drink.'

'No, thanks, I don't need one.'

But when he reappeared it was with a wine glass in one hand, and a glass of whisky well qualified with water in the other.

'You might not,' he said, 'but I do, and as I never drink alone, you can accompany me. You look as though you could do with something. It's only white wine, dry, with a hint of floral bouquet and a disconcerting note of passion. Heavy day?'

'Not really,' she said, reluctantly accepting the glass. He had made the description of the wine too intimate, too personal, his abrasive voice lingering over the words as though he was applying them to her, not the wine.

'What shall we drink to?' he asked, not trying to hide the note of mockery in his voice.

Eyes the colour and clarity of a topaz searched her face; he seemed to be trying to probe through the skin to the thoughts in her brain, the emotions in her heart.

Determined not to let him see how uncomfortable she was, she said lightly, 'The future is always a good toast. It covers a lot of ground.'

'So it does. Well, Aura Forsythe, here's to the future. May it be all that you need.'

Made gauche by the unexpected wording, she said, 'And yours, too,' and swallowed some of the wine before setting the glass down.

'Do you intend leaving yours to fate?' he asked with apparent disinterest, tilting his glass so that the light refracted in the liquid like a thousand glinting cyrstals, exactly the same shade as his eyes.

'What else can I do?' Picking up a marbled swordleaf of flax, she positioned it carefully, as carefully as she kept her face turned away.

He laughed softly. 'Oh, I believe in making my own future. Somehow I thought you would too.'

'I don't believe one can,' she said, stung by the inference that she was a manipulator.

'Of course you can. There is always the unexpected, but we lay the ground rules.'

'We plan,' she returned crisply. 'But quite often our plans go awry.'

'Not mine,' he said with such assurance that she believed him. 'Not when you know what you're doing. And I make sure I do.'

Aura had always been quick to read signals. The circumstances of her upbringing had honed a natural skill to razor sharpness. His voice was even, without inflection, his eyes hooded in an immobile face, his words laconic, yet the threat was naked and open between them.

'But of course,' he finished almost indifferently, 'you have to understand what you're doing. And gathering information can take a little time.'

Aura moved a chyrsanthemum flower a few centimetres to the right. She had nothing to fear from Flint because there was nothing he could do to hurt her. She loved Paul, and Paul loved her, and because of that, she was safe.

Turning her head, she gave Flint a mocking smile. 'I'm afraid you won't find very much more about me. Apart from my previous two engagements I've lived a fairly dull life. Earnestly middle class, according to my mother.'

His lashes drooped, hiding the dazzling shimmer of his gaze. 'If there's anything to be discovered, I'll find it.'

It was stupid to be so alarmed by a simple statement. But in spite of her confidence, Aura's skin prickled, its tiny hairs pulled upright by an atavistic fear that had no base in logic.

Carefully not looking his way, holding her shoulders straight and high, she stepped back to survey her work. Perhaps the vase needed another chrysanthemum? She sorted through the flowers.

'Leave it,' Flint commanded smoothly, 'it's perfect. A skilful, disciplined piece of work, with just enough surprises to stop it from being boring.'

Ignoring the insinuation, Aura shrugged. 'Thank you,' she said, infusing the polite words with more than a hint of irony. Quickly gathering up the few flowers remaining, she headed purposefully towards the kitchen.

'You left your wine behind,' Flint told her helpfully, following her to put the glass down on the bench.

'I don't drink in the daytime, anyway.' She began to arrange the blooms in a pottery jug.

'That's a very womanly skill. Did you take lessons?'

'No.'

He was lounging against the bench, one hip supporting his lean body, thighs taut as his flat stomach, turning the glass in tanned, long fingers, watching her as though she was something new and intriguing. The impact of his gaze kept her on edge, tightening nerves she had never suspected she had. Outside the rain, dull herald of winter, beat glumly at the windows, washing away the summer and the warm days and cool nights of autumn.

'You surprise me.' His soft voice sent catspaws of sensation through her. 'You're so glossily self-assured, so polished and perfect and finished that I assumed you must have gone to one of those schools in Switzerland where they teach you how to run a mansion and dazzle dowagers and intrigue every man you meet.'

'My mother was sent to one,' she told him indifferently, 'but I wasn't.'

'Why not?'

'My stepfather thought it would be wasted on me.'

At eighteen she had been locked in open battle with Lionel Helswell, and she would have gone anywhwere that would take her away from him. But he had vetoed the plan, in spite of the fact that the fees would have been taken from her trust fund.

He'd been able to forbid her the money because Natalie had said airily that she never understood figures, so she'd signed over the responsibility for everything, including the trust fund, to Lionel. And that upright, small-minded, petty man, with his rectitude and his authoritative air and his rigid ideas of discipline, had spent it all on a sordid secret life of gambling and bought women.

Aura had made sure *she* understood figures, as well as boring bourgeois things like bank statements and balance sheets.

'Didn't the adoring cousin come to light?'

Aura's shoulders straightened. 'Alick had nothing to do with it,' she said crisply.

'But he paid for you to go to university, didn't he?' Flint's voice was unhurried but relentless.

Aura bit her lip. 'Yes,' she said reluctantly.

As always Lionel had refused any support, so she had let Alick stake her on the understanding that she would pay him back. At a polytechnical college in parklike grounds in the west of Auckland she had begun to study accountancy so she would never be at the financial mercy of any man again. Somewhat to her suprise she had discovered that she liked working with figures and with money; at least it didn't make emotional demands on her.

However, before long she had been lured into tackling a double major in information systems and marketing, which she had enjoyed immensely.

'So you spent as long as you could there,' he said coolly. 'It took you four years—did you play too much to get your papers in the conventional three?'

Aura stared at him. Didn't he know that she had done a double major? No, clearly he didn't. His vaunted information retrieval system had let him down badly! He probably thought she had frolicked around university looking for a husband. And she certainly wasn't going to tell him that she had spent most of her time with her nose to the grindstone.

'I enjoyed myself,' she admitted.

They had been happy, worthwhile, busy years, full of fun and hard work. She had lived in a succession of small flats with other students close to campus, and during the holidays she had worked long hours to pay Alick back, so she had seen very little of Lionel.

He had hated the fact that she was out of his control. The thought made her mouth tuck up.

'You have a maddening smile,' Flint remarked casually. 'Secretive and dangerous and infinitely alluring. No wonder Paul fell so heavily.'

'We love each other.' Her voice was cool and devoid of any emotion but confidence. Flint Jansen was a bully, and the only way to deal with bullies was to keep calm and detached. 'But I'm sure the dossier you have on me must tell you that.'

'No,' he returned, his eyes narrowed intently beneath the screen of his lashes. 'It tells me that each man you've been engaged to has been richer than the last, and that you dumped each one only after you'd met the next poor fool. Your last ex is still licking his wounds. You and your pretty, conniving, useless mother are on the bones of your backside now, with no money to cushion your fall from grace, so I imagine Paul was a godsend. Rich, adoring, and ready to take on your parasite of a mother, too.'

'I don't have to put up with this kind of thing,' she said icily.

His smile was just as cold. 'Yes, you do,' he said with arrogant confidence, 'because I'm not letting you go until you've listened to everything I have to say.'

Anger bit into her, anger and a deep, clawing fear that shredded the restraint she had worked so hard to build over the years. She said in a voice that trembled slightly, 'I don't know why you took such an instant dislike to me——'

He laughed, a low, harsh sound that ripped at her nerves. 'Don't lie, Aura. You know; you're just not admitting it.'

Her green eyes flew to meet his. Did that mean—yes, he was looking at her with contemptuous understanding, the corners of his hard mouth curling.

'For exactly the same reason that you took such an instant dislike to me,' he went on, holding her gaze effortlessly, drowning her in fire. 'When I looked into those great green eyes with their dancing golden specks and saw the false smile that rested so easily on your delectable mouth, I realised that you're certainly not in love with Paul. Because you want to go to bed with me, Aura.'

CHAPTER THREE

AURA flinched as though she had been slapped in her turn.

'You must be the most conceited man I've ever met,' she said, contempt coating every syllable. 'What the hell makes you think that I'd choose you over Paul?'

She let her eyes strip him down in a slow, scornful survey, so caught up in her need to convince him that she failed to notice the sudden, dangerous tension on the big body she was insolently undressing with her eyes.

'You might be taller than he is,' she said relentlessly, 'but brute force has never interested me much. I look for different things in men.'

'Money, according to your mother.'

Aura froze. 'What——?'

'I had lunch with Natalie today.'

He was speaking softly, consideringly, yet his voice blocked out the sound of the rain outside, the thunder of her heart in her ears. But not the astonishment. Apart from a few select luncheons with close friends Natalie hadn't been out of the unit since they'd moved in. A swift pang of betrayal tore through Aura. Oh, Natalie, she thought wearily.

That piercing shaft of emotion slipped the leash of her temper. 'You seem to have a liking for prying and probing and sticking your nose into other people's business,' she retorted on a rising note of anger, green sparks glittering in her eyes.

At least the subject was no longer her unbidden response to his physical maleness.

51

His smile was pure mockery. 'I'm a concerned and caring human being.'

'I'm sure it does you credit.' Reining in her emotions, she looked him fair and square in the face. 'What really concerns you? The loss of Paul's friendship? But you must have known that he would marry one day. Unless you hoped that he had other inclinations.'

Apparently not in the least upset by the sneering insinuation, his smile turned masculine and predatory. 'I'm heterosexual, Aura, just as Paul is. As I said last night, if you understand the concept of friendship at all, you should be able to accept that I'd do almost anything in my power to keep him from the clutches of a greedy little tramp who's been brought up to use her sexy body and beautiful face as a commodity, trading exclusive access to it for money and security.'

Of course he'd used the word tramp again deliberately, but this time she refused to react. He was some distance away but it was still too close. She saw him even when she wasn't looking at him, felt his presence at some deep cellular level, and was afraid of her intense awareness. And of the bleak bitterness that submerged her legendary temper.

Shoving the blue pottery jug to the back of the bench, she said curtly, 'If that's what you think of me, it's no use my trying to convince you otherwise. I'm going now.'

It was a retreat. Craven, cowardly, yet she knew that she was doing the right thing. Flint's presence sent every nerve in her body dancing a crazy jig. He had threatened her, and she was going to run away; Aura had never backed down in her life before, but instinct warned her that she was at a disadvantage when it came to dealing with this man.

Half-closed eyes gleaming golden slivers, he said, 'I thought the caterers were coming to prepare for tonight.'

She bit her lip. 'You could let them in.'

His smile was arrogantly outlined. 'I could, but I'm sure they need instructions.'

Of course they did. Aura's mouth tightened as she nodded.

With no more than a hint of cynical amusement in his tone, he said, 'Finish your drink, and after you've told them what to do I'll take you home.'

Fortunately they turned up then, and after ten minutes' consultation Aura was able to leave. To her dismay Flint insisted on driving her back, but at least he didn't initiate any conversation. Not that his silence soothed Aura's stretched nerves or eased the panic that crawled like an obscene beast beneath her brittle composure, but she was grateful for it, nevertheless, and even more grateful to find that Natalie was still out.

He didn't come in and she closed the door with a relief that left her weak and shaking. The shrill jangle of the telephone made her jump; her hand shook as she picked up the receiver and her cousin's deep, pleasant voice almost brought tears to her eyes.

'You sound beleaguered,' he said. 'Is Natalie playing up again?'

'No.' She swallowed the hot words of complaint that came to her lips. She was grown-up now, and Alick had other loyalties. 'I think I must be indulging in that well-known syndrome, bride's nerves,' she said, trying to sound cheerful.

'You're entitled. Would you like Laurel to come over?'

'No, I'm just being silly. Have you arrived, or are you still in Kerikeri?'

'We got to the apartment ten minutes ago. What time do you want us to pick you up?'

Automatically Aura began to refuse, but Alick was accustomed to getting his own way, and when she hung up she had agreed to go the party with them.

Almost immediately afterwards Natalie came in, sleek and laughing. Aura wanted to fly at her and demand that she stop seeing Flint, stop talking so freely to him, but of course she didn't. Natalie had every right to go where she wanted and see who she wanted.

Anyway, the lunch was a milestone. At last Natalie was breaking out of the lassitude that had held her victim for so long.

But Aura wasn't able to banish her uneasy apprehension. She had managed to change the direction of Flint's thoughts this afternoon, but only because he had let her. He was going to spoil these weeks before the wedding with his hateful insinuations and his shrewd, too accurate understanding of how her mind worked.

Still, she had coped with Lionel Helswell; she could cope with Flint Jansen. The thought didn't exactly cheer her, but it did summon a militant sparkle to her great eyes.

All too soon it was time to get ready. Aura chose a black georgette skirt she had had for years and a black silk blouse of about the same vintage. With it she teamed a jacket the green of her eyes, and a pair of Chanel earrings.

'I don't know why you won't buy something new,' Natalie complained. 'Honestly, Aura, you're taking this economy drive too far. It's just ridiculous. When you're married Paul will pay for your clothes—why not now?'

'Humour me,' Aura returned with a tight smile.

'Oh, you're impossible,' her mother wailed. 'At least you could have bought something to wear tonight.'

'I have got new clothes——'

'Nothing really chic!'

'There's not a great call for chic on a tropical beach.'

Natalie sighed ostentatiously. The sound of a car drawing up outside did little to brighten her expression. Natalie didn't like Alick, and had no time at all for Laurel, his wife.

However, she showed no signs of her dislike when they came in, and after the greetings they set off, to all intents a very cheerful party. Except that behind Aura's laughter there was a dark cloud which had settled into place the first time Flint Jansen looked into her eyes.

In spite of her forebodings the party seemed set to go off really well. Paul was his usual charming and hospitable self, everyone was determined to have a good time, and there already existed that indefinable atmosphere which marked off the merely successful party from the one that would be remembered for years.

It should have been a happy occasion for Aura; this was the first time she had ever acted as Paul's hostess and she was determined to get it right. But the strain of keeping her eyes away from Flint as he moved around the room, and the fear that somehow he could sense her almost avid interest in him, kept her on edge. There was a mechanical quality to her smile and her greetings, a hidden, unhappy tension that wouldn't be banished.

However, he stayed well away from her, not even looking her way, and after half an hour or so she almost relaxed. Until her bridesmaid arrived, cast a look around the room and stiffened, for all the world, Aura thought tartly, like a bird-dog sighting game.

Jessica moaned, 'Oh, God, who is the hunk?'

'The best man. Flint Jansen.' The words were clipped and without expression.

'You mean I get to walk down the aisle beside him? Lucky, lucky me.' Jessica turned the three words into a lascivious growl. 'Oh, I love men like that.'

'Like what?'

'Dangerous as hell. The sort of man who makes you think of pirates and reckless adventurers and arrogant, haughty Regency rakes. A man who expects the world to adjust to him, and gets away with it because we just can't resist men with that casual, in-built authority. Oh, wouldn't I enjoy six months on a desert island with him!'

'Nobody,' Aura observed mildly, 'would believe that you're engaged to a man you show every sign of loving. What does Sam say when you drool over men like this?'

Jessica laughed. 'Nothing. He knows I've never gone from looking to touching.' She eyed Flint with appreciation that held more than a hint of speculation.

'Isn't he worried that you might?'

Her best friend snorted. 'When would I get the time? Building up a modelling agency doesn't leave me any time for playing around, believe me. Besides, I love Sam, even if he is always off on business trips. Flint Jansen is not the sort of man it's safe to love, or even play with. He has a distinctly untamed look, and I'll bet he's hell on his women.'

'I bow to your superior knowledge,' Aura snapped.

Jessica looked sagaciously at her. 'Does Paul know you're a virgin?'

'Yes.'

'Good.' Jessica hesitated, then said cautiously, 'You know it doesn't always work out perfectly the first time, don't you?'

Touched, Aura laughed. 'Yes, mother hen. I know quite a lot about it, actually. I haven't exactly had my head stuffed under a pillow since I grew old enough to read novels and magazines.'

'Theoretical knowledge is not the same as the real thing, but you'll be all right. Paul's a dear, and he's not going to rip your clothes off and take you in a storm of uncontrollable passion.' Jessica's eyes moved from Paul's face to that of the man beside him. 'But I'll bet his best man could, if he felt like it.'

Something hungry and feral moved in the pit of Aura's stomach. Appalled by her body's betrayal, she said, 'He looks very self-possessed to me. Not the sort to lose his head.'

'Yep, but imagine if you were able to breach those barriers. Wow!'

Abruptly, Aura said, 'Sometimes you talk an awful lot of rot.'

'True.' As though compelled, Jessica's eyes followed Flint around. 'You know, he's just gorgeous. That scar really does something, doesn't it. I wonder how he got it. Not that it matters—it's terribly evocative and buccaneerish. I wonder if he'd be interested in modelling. He moves like a dream, too. If the camera likes him he'd be perfect.'

For some reason the suggestion irritated Aura. 'He's too busy haring off around the world saving Robertson's from assorted villains who want to snitch some of their profits. Come on, Mrs McAlpine is looking a little lost.'

'Hmm. How are things going there?'

Aura shrugged. 'She still doesn't think I'm good enough for her darling son, but it's not personal; she doesn't think anyone's good enough.'

Even if the older woman had reservations until the day she died, Aura wasn't going to worry about her. She knew she could make Paul happy.

An hour later she was dancing in his arms, waiting for the sense of security, the deep inner contentment that Paul's touch, his presence, his dearness, had always given her.

It didn't come. Oh, she felt safe. She also felt empty, alone.

Her teeth sank a moment into her full bottom lip. Of course she was strung up; all brides were. It went with the territory. It was practically indecent not to wonder whether you were making a mistake.

That was why she wasn't able to respond to Paul as quickly as usual. Forcing her body to relax, she let her eyelids droop until the rest of the room was just a blur of light and colour and movement.

Laughter, low and intimate, grated across her ear. When she lifted her lashes a fraction she saw Jessica's slender form in Flint's embrace. In spite of Sam's absence, Jessica was enjoying herself. Or perhaps she was drumming up business for her agency.

From the predatory glint in Flint's eyes, he didn't find it at all hard to hold Jessica far too closely. Not that many men would. She looked just what she was, a smart, sophisticated businesswoman, but as well as being beautiful, she was intelligent and kind and fun.

Aura was stabbed by an emotion so intense that it felt like a spear ripping through her flesh. To her horror, she realised it was jealousy.

'That was a big sigh.' Paul's voice, with his smile evident in it, caressed her ear.

'Mmm.' She snuggled into him, tilting her chin a little defiantly when she caught his mother's eye.

'You'll be able to sleep in tomorrow. And in a couple of weeks' time, darling, you can spend as much time in bed as you like.' His voice was soft and significant.

Aura suddenly found herself wishing they hadn't decided not to make love until they were married. Not that it had been a joint decision. When he realised just how afraid and wary she was Paul had told her understandingly that he could wait.

Now she wondered whether, if that hurdle had been surmounted, she'd be aching with forbidden desire for another man. Almost certainly the act of loving would have sealed their commitment to each other, and she would be confident and unashamed, not tormented by a shameful need that burrowed secretly beneath the shining surface of her self-esteem.

A poem of Blake's came to her mind; he might have written it for her.

O Rose, thou art sick!
The invisible worm
That flies in the night,
In the howling storm,
Has found out thy bed

Of crimson joy:
And his dark secret love
Does thy life destroy.

The attraction she felt for Flint ate into the fabric of
her love like a worm, spoiling it.

'Mmm,' she murmured huskily, knowing it for a lie.
'Sounds good.'

'Darling, it will be more than good, I promise you.'

He kissed her hair, but all Aura could concentrate on
was Jessica's laughter, breathy, knowing. Jealousy and
a bitter resentment of the woman she had called friend
for more than half her life ate into her composure.

Then, thank heaven, the music stopped. Aura pulled
away from Paul and, without looking at the other two,
began to walk towards the stereo.

'No, your cousin's putting on another tape,' Paul said,
sliding an arm around her waist.

Aura stiffened; an instinctive withdrawal darkened her
eyes, blocked her throat. Alick had chosen something
smooth and slow, a sentimental ballad touched in places
with salt, sung by a soprano with a voice like bitter choc-
olate. Steeling herself to relax, Aura moved back into
Paul's embrace.

But, smiling above her head, he said, 'I think we
should swap partners, Flint. I want to find out just what
Sam's up to.'

He looked down at Aura just too late to catch the
feverish dismay that flared in her eyes before being
swiftly hidden by long, thick lashes.

She couldn't shake her head, she couldn't shout at
him for being so unperceptive, she couldn't stamp and
grind her teeth and yell as she used to when she was a
child; she had to smile, and smile some more, and let
Flint Jansen take her into his arms.

It was a revelation, an explosion of the senses. His
smooth animal grace and controlled vitality made him

a superb dancer, but that wasn't what set her body springing to life. It seemed to Aura as though light streamed through her, filling her with the sparks that sunlight summoned from her diamond, lifting her into a rarefied region where gravity no longer held its ponderous sway.

Her reactions became keener, more acute. Her nostrils were teased by a faint fragrance of male, infinitely exciting, infinitely tantalising. The material of his jacket beneath her fingers was suddenly *there*; before, she had barely noticed it, but now its smooth matt texture intrigued her fingertips. And Flint's hand around hers was warm and firm and strong, the long fingers holding hers loosely yet with an assurance that sent flutters of sensation along her nerves.

The heat in the pit of her stomach burst into flames, urging her body into instant life, an awareness which was barbaric in its intensity, violent, miraculous.

Her eyes were dazzled by the whiteness of his shirt against the fine black material of his dinner jacket. How well the austere garb suited his big, lean body; it should have clothed his potently male charisma in conventionality, but instead the contrast heightened it.

'You're very quiet.' His voice was low and amused, its sexy roughness abrading every nerve and cell inside her.

'I'm tired.' It was the only excuse she could think of. She would die if he realised the effect he had on her. Her only hope was to stay silent until the dance had finished and she could get away from him and the overwhelming, totally terrifying response he summoned.

'Arranging flowers exhausts you?'

She smiled weakly and didn't answer.

'Or perhaps it's too many late nights?'

The razor slash of sarcasm in his voice startled her. Even as she told herself not to do it, she glanced up.

He was watching her with fire smouldering in the crystalline depths of his eyes, a fire that was immediately extinguished, yet she recognised it, because the same dark fire had burned inside her when she'd heard Jessica laugh in his arms.

It was sexual jealousy, primitive and unrestrained, as harsh as an Antarctic winter, as hot as a solar flare.

A fierce exultation almost loosened her tongue, but she curbed it. Her defences against this destructive, cataclysmic response were few and puny. Silence, passive resistance, was all that she had.

And her honour. She had pledged her love to Paul. She was not going to break that vow, not for the meretricious fool's gold of sexual attraction.

'No,' she said remotely. 'Brides are supposed to exhaust themselves. It's part of the mystique.'

'I don't know much about brides.' His voice was bland, as though he had a secret amusement he wasn't going to share.

Yet her sharpened senses told her that he was not impervious, that he was just as stimulated as she was by their closeness. 'Never been married?' she asked steadily.

'Never.'

'Did you and Paul make some sort of vow of bachelorhood?' She used Paul's name deliberately, trying to dampen down the strain that sizzled between them.

Flint's ironic laughter sent a febrile shiver down her backbone. 'No. I'm away too much to make for a good marriage.'

Some of Natalie's teachings came into her head. Men liked to talk about themselves, about their jobs. It just might save her now. 'What exactly do you do?'

His shoulders moved. 'I mend fences,' he said. 'If they're irrevocably damaged, I stop too many sheep from falling over the cliff.'

'That tells me nothing except that you grew up on a farm, and I already knew that.'

'My job's not for discussion. Besides, I'm thinking of giving it up.'

Her upwards glance caught a strange look on the tough, hard-honed features. She'd swear that Flint was just as surprised at what he'd said as she was. 'Are you going to swallow the anchor?' she asked lightly. 'Take a desk job?'

'No.' His hesitation lasted barely a second. 'I'll make wine.'

Aura missed a step. 'Wine?' It seemed an odd career for a man who earned his living in various hot spots around the globe, some of them very dangerous indeed, if Paul was to be believed.

'My great-grandfather was a vintner,' Flint said. 'He grew grapes and made his own wine. I want to produce a red wine as good as those they make in France.'

He was smiling, she could hear it in his voice, and she was seized by a stupid, unattainable desire to have him smile at her without any agenda, openly, frankly.

'That's every winemaker's ambition, surely,' she said, more to hear what he had to say than to object. If Flint said he was going to give French winegrowers a run for their money, she believed him. He was that sort of man. Success was written in his face, in the way he walked and moved.

'It won't be the same as those they grow in France,' he said, taking her point immediately. 'It will be different, because the climate and the soil are different, but it will be a world-class wine, nevertheless.'

'Why red?' she asked, intrigued. 'We produce some of the best white wines in the world; why not make them?'

The wide shoulders moved a little beneath her hand. 'The challenge is in the reds.'

Yes, he'd want a challenge.

'I know they're growing superb wines in all sorts of places in New Zealand now, even in Otago, where you'd think it would be far too cold. Where will you go?'

'I've got land just north of Auckland,' he said, almost indifferently. 'It's perfect for growing wine with character. A hundred acres on a peninsula with an estuary and a river on three sides, soil that's iron sandstone with clay, an ideal climate, hot days and cool nights and some fairly ferocious frosts in winter, and a range of hills to keep off the worst of the winds.'

'Doesn't it rain too much there?'

'Not according to the climate charts.' The aloofness had vanished from his voice, replaced by an enthusiasm he couldn't conceal.

'And what do you know about making wine?' she asked with interest.

'Quite a lot,' he said, 'but I have a French friend who wants to get away from a tricky family situation, and he's an expert. Between us we'll show the world that it's not only the Australians who can produce good red wine in the South Pacific.'

'It sounds fascinating,' she said.

'Hard work,' he returned dismissively, glancing down at her with a sardonic amusement that raised her hackles. 'And very little money for years, if ever. A life on the land is not at all romantic. It's sheer slog, often expensively frustrating, with the weather and everything else against you. You're a high-flyer, too polished, too finished, to be able to settle down in some small country area.'

His insulting opinion shouldn't hurt, but it did. She had to force herself to smile up at him, watching with a secret, passionate pleasure the slow darkening of his golden gaze, the tiny muscle that flicked a betrayal against the harsh sweep of his jawbone. Yes, he felt it too, the wildfire need that swept like silken doom through her veins. Recognised it, and resented it as much as she did.

And then, thank heavens, the music stopped, and she pulled free of his arms.

'Thank you,' he murmured, smiling dangerously, hooded eyes concealing his emotions.

Ten minutes later, once more safely in Paul's arms, she saw him dancing with a cousin of Paul's whose name she couldn't remember. The tall, lovely blonde was gazing into his eyes with open, acquisitive eagerness.

To hide the obscure pang of pain that sawed through her Aura said on a half laugh, 'It looks as though your best man's made a conquest.'

Paul laughed. 'I'd have been surprised if he hadn't. Ever since he was fourteen Flint's only had to walk into a room to have half the women in it make eyes at him.'

Aura said dismissively, 'It's that macho air. Some women find it impossible to resist.'

'But not you?'

She lifted her brows at him. 'Well, I can see why he attracts interest,' she said, trying to sound objective and sensible. 'Alick's got it too, that inner hardness, a sort of toughness of mind and character. It's exciting, but it takes a rare woman to cope with it. I want other things in my husband.'

His mouth quirked into a smile. Aura sensed that she had disappointed him, but she would not lie to him. 'Some time you must tell me what they are,' he murmured, his eyes on her mouth.

Her smile was demure. Oh, she loved him, loved him for all the things Flint didn't pretend to; she loved him because he was kind, because he was tender and thoughtful and safe, and because he loved her. Set against all that, what did Flint have to offer but a wild thundering in the blood that would inevitably lead to disillusion? Men like Flint were too arrogantly masculine for safe taming.

'Some time in the not too distant future,' she promised, fluttering her lashes upward in a parody of flirtatiousness, 'I will.'

His arms contracted around her. He was aroused, and for one paralysing second Aura wanted to twist away from the telltale hardness of his body. As though he understood, he held her only for a moment before gently releasing her.

'I'll look forward to it,' he said softly, the words a vow.

An hour later she and Jessica were sitting in a corner of the room, discussing a few minor, last minute details about the wedding.

'I really think I've covered everything,' Aura said with a sigh. 'I just hope there aren't too many snags.'

'Oh, it'll be a howling success,' Jessica assured her confidently. 'You've always been efficient and sensible, and you've got the knack for making an occasion fun. Look at tonight. Most pre-wedding parties are horrors, with both sides of the family eyeing each other up in affronted astonishment, and the friends wondering how on earth they're going to see the evening out. But everyone's having a marvellous time, and that's due to you. You make people want to enjoy themselves.'

'I was well taught.' Aura's roving gaze rested on her mother, flirting with one of Paul's widowed uncles.

Mrs McAlpine was watching them too, clearly unhappy with the situation. She needn't get her plaits in a tangle, Aura thought cynically. Natalie liked all the preliminaries to flirting, the sideways glances, the hammering pulses and slow, significant pauses, the magical meeting of eyes. Her great beauty ensured that she indulged frequently in such byplay, but she never followed through. She was essentially a frigid woman. If she married again, it would be to have a man about the house—rich, naturally—not for the pleasure of his lovemaking.

Her maternal grandfather, Aura decided, not for the first time, had a lot to answer for.

For a while Aura had assumed that her mother's deep-seated inner coldness was hereditary. Then she had met Paul, and her worries had almost dissipated. Almost, but not quite.

It was bitterly ironic that it should be the best man who finally routed her fears. She wasn't unresponsive in Flint's arms; she damned near burst into flames.

'Who's the woman dancing with Flint? The tall blonde with the hungry eyes?'

Aura shrugged, keeping her eyes fixed on her mother. 'Paul's cousin, Belinda somebody.'

'She's certainly not trying to hide how she feels, is she? It's a wonder she doesn't just throw him down on the floor and have her way with him here and now.'

'Here?' Aura concealed her raw emotions with a caustic inflection. 'Don't be silly, Mrs McAlpine would disown her.'

'Wouldn't she just! A very proper lady, your mother-in-law.'

'Future mother-in-law.'

Jessica sent a sideways glance towards her. 'OK,' she said amiably. 'Future it is.'

They relapsed into silence. Unwillingly, Aura watched Belinda laugh at Flint, press her long, curvaceous body against him as they turned, and once more had to fight back a tide of corroding jealousy. Jessica's voice was a welcome relief.

'Paul and Flint don't seem to have anything in common, do they? It's odd that they're still such great friends,' Jessica said thoughtfully. 'Even after——'

She stopped, an odd occurrence for Jessica whose tact was notorious.

'Even after what?' Aura stared at her friend.

Jessica shrugged uncomfortably. 'My big mouth! You'd think I'd learn, wouldn't you? Oh, hell, apparently it's common knowledge. Drusilla Evans told me. Yes, I know she gossips, but you must admit her gossip is usually accurate. She said that a couple of years ago Flint more or less walked off with one of Paul's girlfriends. Mind you, it can't have gone deep, because they still remained friends.'

A movement from behind caught the corner of Aura's eye. She recognised Paul, and wondered sickly whether he had heard. Swiftly she said, 'Gossip is gossip, and none of it's worth believing.'

But in her mind she saw Flint as a predator, taking what he wanted without worrying—no, that was silly, it was wrong, because he was very concerned about Paul. Guilty conscience, perhaps? *No*!

Jessica bit her lip and fell silent as Paul came up and slid his arm around Aura's waist. 'Everything's going like a dream,' he said. 'You've done wonders. Hasn't she, Jessica?'

'I was just telling her so.' After a worried glance at Aura, Jessica launched into a very funny story about a party she had attended the week before, and soon the disquiet was dissipated in the nicest manner, by laughter.

But later, when they were dancing again, Paul said abruptly, 'I heard what Jessica was telling you, and it didn't happen quite the way she thinks. I'm not such a wimp that I'd let Flint get away with stealing a girlfriend.'

Aura's brows shot up. 'Did either of you consider,' she asked with tart emphasis, 'that the girlfriend may have felt that she was in control of her actions, not just an object to be stolen or kept?'

Paul grinned unrepentantly. 'My little feminist! All right, but Jessica used the word first. Anyway, Gemma fell out of love with me and into love with Flint, who was not interested in her.'

'An awkward situation.' Aura spoke without expression. Something in Paul's tone, in the way he had brought the matter up, convinced her that Gemma's defection had mattered very much.

'Yes. I was cool to Flint—well, I knew it wasn't his fault, but until I met you she was the one woman I'd thought I loved. And I don't think I could have borne it if Flint had been in love with her. It would have seemed like the rankest betrayal, which is stupid, of course.'

'Well, yes, it is a bit, because none of us is exactly in control of our emotions,' Aura said gently, for the first time in her life understanding with an acid clarity how true this was, 'but it must have hurt. In a funny sort of way I felt the same when Alick and Laurel got married. Alick had been my substitute brother, and I'd got into the habit of relying on him. Then Laurel came along, and although he was still there for me, I knew that nothing was ever going to be quite the same again. I despised myself for being jealous, but it didn't stop it.'

He gave her a quick spontaneous hug. 'I do love you,' he said. 'My sensible angel. Somehow you've robbed the whole thing of its last nasty little sting.'

Hidden beneath the affection and the respect, Paul nurtured a deep envy of his friend, envy of the raw sensuality that emanated from Flint, the stark, uncompromising maleness that was at once a threat and a challenge to every woman who saw him.

Paul's unexpected vulnerability shook her. Aura loved him at that moment more than ever. He must never know of that unwanted, savage tug of attraction, not even after it had been dissipated to nothingness by time and familiarity and the real gold of her love for Paul.

A quick glance across the room revealed Flint still dancing with Belinda, smiling down at her lovely face with lazy approval. As though Aura's gaze was tangible, he looked up, transfixing her with the golden fire of his eyes, then deliberately turned away. Whatever he said into Belinda's ear made her bridle and flush.

Sheer, black rage, the like of which she had never experienced before, fountained through Aura, terrifying her with its strength. She wanted to tear Belinda from Flint's arms and throw her out of the room, out of the apartment into the dark, wet night, and she wanted to slap him senseless. How dared he smile like that at another woman?

She fought a vicious battle for victory over the vulgar, indiscriminate desire that held her prisoner. Slowly, laboriously, she used her considerable willpower to banish the bastard emotion so that common sense could reassert itself.

Although she succeeded, it took even more effort to force herself to smile and talk and behave normally, to pretend that nothing was wrong, that she was the same as she had always been. Inside her psyche some fundamental shift had taken place, some rearrangement of her inner self, and she didn't know how to defend herself against the shaming, painful flaw that marred her self-image as surely as the scar marred Flint's face.

Except, she thought acidly, somehow he managed to turn even that into an asset. The cruel mark that would have disfigured anyone else merely emphasised his elemental attraction.

The evening wore down. By two in the morning everyone had gone, even Alick and Laurel, Paul having announced his intention of taking Aura home. Glowing and sweetly mischievous, Natalie had left an hour before with Paul's uncle, and Mrs McAlpine had been driven home by the extremely reluctant Belinda, who at the last moment had kissed Flint with obvious enjoyment. An enjoyment, Aura realised with sick self-derision, he had reciprocated.

'I shouldn't be long,' Paul said, looking ironically at his friend. 'Don't wait up for me, though.'

Flint's teeth showed briefly in the smile that made Aura think of a hungry tiger, burnished and gleaming in a tropical forest. She almost flinched; only the armour she had spun out of determination kept her outwardly serene, although it didn't protect her from the maelstrom of emotions the evening had unleashed.

Until she had seen Flint smile into Belinda's face she had been more or less in control of her feelings and her life. Her poise had been hard-won, and secretly she was rather proud of it.

But that openly sexual smile had wrenched it all away, torn free the shield of her restraint and revealed in all their wildness and untamed greed the desires that prowled beneath the thin veneer of civilised reserve.

Instinct warned Aura that nothing was ever going to be the same again.

She was caught in a trap from which there was no escape, the trap of her own needs and desires. Oh, she loved Paul, but, set against the primitive sensations Flint roused in her, love didn't seem to be enough.

Rationalise it however she did, she was in trouble. If Flint came back to New Zealand and started up his vineyard just north of Auckland they would see quite a bit of him. Although Paul made friends easily, his loyalty was to the old friends with whom they did most of their socialising. Yes, she would certainly see Flint, and this ache of longing wouldn't die of starvation.

'You're very quiet,' Paul murmured in the car.

She shrugged, staring out through the windscreen. Rain dashed down, was smoothed away by the rhythmic sweep of the wipers. Street-lights danced in the drops. 'I hate winter,' she said dully.

'Waste of emotion. It comes, and eventually it goes. And admit it, darling, it's not always like this. We get glorious weather as often in winter as we do in any other season. It's just cooler.'

She sighed. 'Mmm.'

'What's worrying you?'

'Nothing.' What else could she say?

I want to go to bed with your best man and best friend? No, I don't love him, I don't even like him much, but when he looks at me I get these strange sensations in my body and I don't know what to do.

A sudden shiver shot down her spine. She yawned. 'It went off well, didn't it?'

'Yes, but I knew it would. You're an excellent hostess.' One hand covered hers briefly, squeezed, and was withdrawn.

Nice hands, she thought, looking at them on the wheel with horrifying detachment. He was a nice man, well made, attractive, sexy in a wholesome way.

Her teeth tightened on her lip, cutting through the thin outer layers of skin. What the hell was she going to do?

At the unit he came in, looking about him with concealed distaste. 'I wish you'd let me move you into the new flat,' he said.

Aura smiled. 'So does Mother.'

'I'll bet. Are you going to make me a cup of coffee?'

They talked of the party, of other things, comfortable, relaxed, and when the coffee was drained he turned her into his arms. Aura held her face eagerly for the kiss, and it was nice. He kissed her gently, then a little less gently, but when she pressed herself against him in an agony, trying to summon the quick leap of the flesh she had felt in Flint's arms, nothing happened.

Paul's lips lingered on the smooth curve of her shoulder. There was no covetousness in his kiss, yet Aura's skin crawled. He laughed softly, and she realised that he had mistaken her shiver for one of anticipation.

'No,' he said, straightening up, 'I'm too old for making love on a sofa with your mother in the next room. I can wait.'

Half of her was pleased, as though she had been threatened, then reprieved. The other half was wretched. She needed reassurance. If they had already been lovers this lightning flash of craving, this rage of sensation would have been satisfied, and she wouldn't ache every time she thought of Flint.

But of course Paul was right. Now was not the time, or the place.

She couldn't sleep. Every quarter hour the chimes of the ponderous old clock that took up far too much room in the flat's small sitting-room resounded in her ear. Normally she never heard it.

After dawn came in, grey and wet and intrusive, she managed to drift into an uneasy doze that was interrupted almost immediately by the shrill stridulation of the telephone.

It was Paul. 'Darling, I've just got a rather panic-stricken call from that firm I'm acting for in Samoa. They want me up there for a day or two to clear up a small mess.'

'You're a solicitor! I thought it was Flint who was the troubleshooter,' she muttered, rubbing sleep from the corner of her eyes.

He laughed. 'And so he is, infinitely more glamorous than I am, I can assure you. Respectable partners in respectable law firms act as troubleshooters in an entirely different way. This is just to tidy up a case I've been working on for some months. There's no derring-do or danger involved. Flint would find it incredibly boring. It's just that things have moved a little more quickly than we expected, and they need help now.'

'But it's the weekend!'

'Which is why I want to get up there today. Tomorrow is a day of rest, and no one will be talking then. Don't be cross, sweetheart. I'll be home on Tuesday, Wednesday at the latest.'

As cheerfully as she could, she said, 'Of course you must go. Just don't dare be called away when we're on our honeymoon!'

'I'll make sure of that,' he said tenderly. 'In two weeks and nine hours, darling, we'll be married, and nobody will be able to tear me from your side.'

Ice coagulated in her stomach. She felt as though he'd thrown her to the wolves, which was completely ridiculous, because she didn't need to see anything of Flint Jansen while Paul was away. Briskly she said, 'Enjoy the sun.'

'Not without you.'

I need you, she screamed silently as she belied her emotions by replacing the receiver very gently. Damn it, how can you go away when I need you here now?

CHAPTER FOUR

Was Paul blind? If he loved her, surely he could sense the anguish she was enduring?

But of course that was unfair, because she was doing her best to hide her emotions from everyone. Even herself.

Especially herself.

And they weren't emotions, they were a simple matter of hormones. Physical attraction, she thought grimly, was like a cold: inconvenient but not fatal.

On her way to the kitchen she glanced through the window. Judging by the lighter sky in the east, the depression that had kept them drenched these last days might finally be on the move. The possibility should have lifted her spirits.

She made coffee and ate a slice of toast, deliberately keeping her mind off everything but the most mundane thoughts. The newspaper had little of interest in it, but her glance fell on a review that made her bite her lip. An Australian Opera Company had brought *The Pearl Fishers* to Auckland for two weeks, and she and Paul were booked to go and see it that night. Opera was not her favourite form of music, but she had been looking forward to this one.

'Oh, damn,' she mumbled, folding the paper up with quick, savage movements.

Hoping the sun might lift her mood, she went out into the garden and began to weed the front border. It was still too wet; great clumps of earth clung defiantly to each root ball, but valiant green spears of daffodil and jonquil leaves were pushing their way through and she could no longer resist their mute appeal.

At eleven o'clock Natalie came strolling out to collect the mail. 'What are you doing, you stupid girl?' she demanded. 'You'll ruin your nails.'

'I'm wearing gloves.' But Aura got to her feet. The small bed was clean and free of clogging growth. 'Look, there are all sorts of bulbs coming up.'

'We won't be here long enough to see the flowers,' Natalie said, dismissing them without even looking.

She was fond of saying that she liked gardens but not gardening. Aura had long realised that her mother liked gardens as a background to her beauty, and adored flowers as gifts not for their own sakes, but because they were homage.

'Sometimes I think you set out to make things difficult,' Natalie complained over her shoulder as she bent down to collect the mail. 'Your nails can still tear, even through gloves, you know. At least you'll be able to afford a gardener when you and Paul decide to buy a house.'

Possibly, but when that happy day came Aura had every intention of doing as much as she could in her own garden. In the meantime she would enjoy the lovely grounds around the apartment block.

They would move when it was time to have children. In the past she had dreamed of Paul's children, but now, even as she smiled, the children who sprang to her mind bore no imprint of the man she loved; they had tiger eyes glowing golden beneath black lashes, and skin bronzed by the summer sun into an antique patina. Instead of Paul's smooth good looks their features were blunt and strong, with wide mouths and high, stark cheekbones and strong jaws. Too energetic to be the handsome children she had imagined before she'd met Flint, they possessed a natural arrogance that translated into their walk and their movements, even the tilt of heads that gleamed with a distinctive copper sheen in the sunlight.

Pain almost overwhelmed her. She was jerked from it by a sharp little sound from her mother. Natalie was thrusting a piece of paper into her pocket, and although her head was turned away, Aura was sure she had gone pale.

'What is it?' she asked brusquely, remembering other occasions when the mail had brought bad news, when mingled with the letters of condolence there had been more and ever more bills.

'Nothing.' Natalie sighed. 'At least, nothing to do with you. An old friend from schooldays has just lost a— grandchild. Oh God, I hate this place! I don't think I'll ever be able to hear the name of this wretched suburb without remembering how miserable I've been here.'

'Well, it won't be for long now,' Aura said gently. She smiled sympathetically down at her maddening, silly mother, who was relying on her to rescue her from these surroundings. All her life someone had looked after Natalie; it was only natural that she expected her daughter to follow suit.

Although, she thought grimly as she followed her mother into the house, the salary she'd get only one year out of university wouldn't go anywhere near satisfying Natalie's needs.

Still, if Aura had been working she wouldn't feel so beholden to Paul, who had waved the magic wand of his love and his wealth and made everything all right.

There were other disadvantages, too. Like the prince in every fairy story, Paul was conventional. He didn't see why his wife should work. Aura had a battle in front of her, but Paul, she thought as she scrubbed her hands, was reasonable. It wouldn't take long for him to understand that she'd go crazy with boredom if she had nothing to do. These last months had been bad enough, but at least she'd had Natalie to look after. Now, with her mother well again, Aura was ready for the challenge of a career.

'Last night was a success,' Natalie said in her most brittle voice. 'A credit to you. Or to me, I suppose, because I taught you.'

Not really. Aunt Helen, who was really a distant cousin, and Alick had been her instructors in social graces and duties, but Aura wasn't unkind enough to point that out. 'I'm glad you enjoyed yourself,' she said instead.

'That brother-in-law of Mary's is rather a dish. He comes from Dunedin. I remember going to his wedding with your father.' Natalie gave a small, sad smile before picking up the latest *Vogue* and riffling through the pages. 'Oh, by the way,' she said after a few minutes, 'Flint rang.'

'Flint?'

'Mm.' Natalie's voice was vague. 'He's going to be out all day, but he said he'd collect you for *The Pearl Fishers* round about six tonight.'

'Flint did?' Aura's voice resounded stupidly in the quiet room.

'Yes. Apparently Paul arranged it.'

Of course. He wouldn't want her to miss a treat. Aura's mouth settled into a hard line. Flint was enough of a hazard to her peace of mind at a distance; spending an evening in his company would be sheer, stupid recklessness.

She waiting a few minutes until her mother went into her bedroom before ringing the apartment. Rather relieved when no one answered, she left a message on the answerphone refusing Flint's kind invitation to take Paul's place. She hoped he couldn't discern the panicky note in her voice.

The early sun was soon banished by another pall of heavy clouds, followed almost immediately by rain. Natalie spent most of the afternoon on her bed, looking weary and as despairing as she had in the months after her husband's death, but refused to admit to anything other than tiredness. There was no sign of the letter that had startled her. However, when afternoon began to thicken into evening, she dragged herself to her feet and decided to take a bath.

'Aren't you going to have one before you go out?' she asked listlessly.

Aura shook her head. 'No. I cancelled.'

Natalie looked at her for a long moment, then nodded. 'Probably a wise decision,' she said.

Aura sat down with a book. She tried hard to concentrate on the words, but Flint's image danced between her eyes and the page, bringing with it that feverish, unbidden excitement. Exhausted by the pull and tug of her emotions, her mind spinning in ever-decreasing circles, she longed to put her head down and slip gratefully into a coma, one that would last long enough for this whole horrible situation to go away.

Except that it wouldn't solve anything. How was it possible to love one man and want another?

'Darling!' Natalie called from the bathroom.

Pleased to be summoned from the dark wasteland of her thoughts, Aura answered mechanically, 'Yes?'

'Get me the bottle of perfume on my dressing-table, will you?'

It was new, and very expensive. Knowing that it was no use complaining, Aura picked it up. Natalie was incapable of resisting the luxuries she had been brought up to consider necessities.

The slam of a car door outside brought Aura's head up. 'I wonder who that can be?'

'Who knows?' Natalie sounded excited, like a child faced with an unexpected treat.

Accustomed to constant entertaining, she used to adore parties and occasions, but it had been months since she had shown any eagerness for a social life. Her interest

'Leaving you and your mother behind. What sort of man was he, to dump his responsibilities like that?' The scorn in his deep voice revealed exactly what he thought of that sort of man.

Aura smiled ironically. 'He was an old-fashioned man like Dr Livingstone, who thought that wives should follow their husbands even if it meant their early death, or their misery.'

'It was unfortunate that his high ideals didn't encompass his wife and child.'

Although Aura had often thought exactly the same thing, she wasn't going to listen to Flint run her father down. With an undertone of warning she said, 'Who knows why other people behave the way they do? I certainly don't judge him.'

'Didn't his departure affect you? Apart from the weeks of crying?'

The question was delivered in a casual tone that didn't fool Aura at all. She shrugged. 'You get over things.'

'How long did you live with Alick Forsythe?'

To her surprise he and Alick had got on well at the party; both powerful men, confident and arrogant. For some reason she hadn't expected them to so clearly enjoy each other's company.

But there was a flick of emotion in his question that snagged her attention. Her eyes scanned the harsh, blunt profile, returning to her hands when she realised that it revealed nothing but strength and a disciplined authority.

In a reserved voice she said, 'I lived in Kerikeri for a couple of years, from ten until I was twelve.' They had been the happiest years of her life.

'Why?'

'Oh, after my father left I ran wild. Natalie couldn't control me.' Natalie didn't really try. 'When she remarried I didn't approve of her choice,' she went on flippantly. 'I had a nice line of tantrums, specialising in high-decibel hysteria. I behaved so badly they sent me

now was an indication of her improvement. An improvement, Aura recognised with a growing dread, that started when she began to go out with Paul.

Slivers of ice attaching themselves to her spine, she frowned at the big Jag that had stopped at the kerb. Yes, that was Flint getting out of it—she'd be able, she thought with painful honesty, to recognise him from a mile away.

For a stupid moment she toyed with the idea of refusing to answer the door, but every light in the place was blazing. And a peremptory knock demanded an answer.

'Hello,' she said coolly, trying to preserve some sort of composure.

He loomed, tall and forbidden and infinitely intimidating; every cell in her body acknowledged his presence.

'Are you wearing those clothes tonight?'

She looked down at her trousers and jersey. 'What's wrong with them?' she asked numbly.

'Nothing, I suppose.' His glittering gaze followed the contours of her body with too much interest.

Aura's breath died in her throat. Her body leapt into vivid life, almost shuddering with a singing anticipation.

'But don't you think,' he went on smoothly, 'that opera demands a little more formality? Especially as we're having dinner first?'

'I'm not——'

'Yes, you are. We don't want to disappoint Paul, do we?'

Torn between a desire so strong she could taste it, sweet and wild and heady, and a fear that drained the light from her eyes and the colour from her skin, Aura said huskily, 'I don't think it would be a good idea, Flint.'

Her shamed glance pleaded with him not to press the matter, but he asked, 'Why not?'

Anger at an obtuseness she knew to be deliberate sparked into life. She retorted crisply, 'I don't really want to go with you. I'm not ready——'

'Then get ready,' he commanded.

He was punishing her, she realised. The momentary flashflame of emotion died into listless fatalism. He looked quite capable of picking her up and carrying her off as though she were some mindless, helpless captive.

'Very well,' she said stiffly, despising herself for capitulating. 'You'd better come in. It will take me twenty minutes or so to get ready.'

Any remote hope she might have had that Natalie would object was extinguished when she came back into the sitting-room. Flint was smiling at her mother, his mouth relaxed into amusement, and Natalie looked better than she had for months, a very becoming colour hinting at her pleasure. When Aura appeared wearing black lace and her grandmother's rare green garnets, her hair restrained in an old-fashioned chignon, her mother smiled almost wistfully.

'Run away and enjoy yourselves,' she said.

Natalie's upbringing, perhaps her nature, had insulated her against the violent tumult of uncontrollable emotions. Her affections were directed very firmly at one person—herself. It would never occur to her that her daughter might feel obliged to call her wedding off because of an inconvenient hang-up over the best man. Paul was much the better bet as a husband, so Natalie, in her own inimitable way, would have been faithful to him.

Aura was not finding it so easy to compartmentalise her life and her inclinations.

Once in the car she sat quietly, refusing to fill the silence with pointless chatter. By forcing her to come out with him, Flint had revealed how little he cared for the usual social conventions, so she wasn't going to indulge in them either.

The front that brought the afternoon rain had m[...] over, and above them a clear sky was spattered with s[...] hazy in the city air. No doubt just north of Auckl[...] where Flint had his land the stars would be huge [...] brilliant, glittering like pale, precious gems in a sky[...] dark and fathomless as black velvet.

Aura adjusted the Edwardian gold and seed-pearl a[...] green garnet bracelet. Its familiar shape and weight [...] her slender wrist should have comforted her, as shoul[...] the heavy warmth of the matching stones in their golde[...] setting around her throat, but she was beyond comfort[...]

Anticipation, forbidden and headily ungovernable,[...] curled like alcohol through her veins, fuzzing her[...] thoughts and kicking in emotions she had never experi-enced before.

Flint said, 'Your father didn't have much to do with[...] your looks, did he?'

'No.' She thought of the father she had never really known. 'He was tall and dark and craggy.'

'What happened to him?'

The smile that curved her lips was sad and angry, b[...] her voice was coolly detached. 'He went to Africa.'

'And left you behind? Why?'

Her shoulders lifted. 'He was a doctor, and he wan[...] to help people who really needed him. I was eight wh[...] he went, and I don't really remember much about[...] except that I cried for weeks afterwards. And ev[...] time——' She stopped.

'And every time——?'

Every time she cried Natalie would stop her[...] wailing long enough to inform her he had left them[...] wasn't coming back because she'd been such a na[...] girl. But she wasn't going to tell Flint that.

Aloud, she said, 'Oh, nothing. He had a dream[...] it wasn't Mother's dream. When she wouldn't g[...] him he went alone.'

to boarding school, but the third time I ran away the school decided I was in need of specialist care and suggested I stay at home while I got it. We had a family conference, and it was agreed that I should live with my Kerikeri cousins.'

'And did you run away from there?'

She laughed. 'Oh, no, that was quite a different kettle of fish. I was an uncivilised little savage, but I knew where I wanted to be. I adored Alick, and his parents, and especially his grandparents, who were darlings but very firm. I soon learnt that tantrums weren't going to succeed, and I stayed put, even when Alick lost his temper with me.'

She had tormented him unmercifully until that happened. Alick's anger had frightened her, but he hadn't hit her, and he hadn't used any of the psychological terrorising that her stepfather was so expert in. That episode had marked the turning point; from then on she had trusted her cousin.

'And you didn't want to go back home?'

She laughed harshly. 'No. Never. I loved it at Kerikeri.'

'I see.' He was silent for a moment, before asking, 'You didn't run away when you went back to boarding school?'

'Nope. I was a reformed child.' Amazing what unconditional love and firm discipline could do.

'What became of your father?'

'He died five years ago, still in Africa. I believe he was happy.'

'You don't know?'

Her shoulders moved an inch. Staring straight ahead she said calmly, 'He didn't write, didn't contact us.'

She had written to him for years, but no reply ever came back. When he left he had cut wife and daughter out of his life as though they had no further meaning for him. Perhaps they hadn't.

'Your stepfather died recently, too, didn't he?' His voice revealed nothing more than mild interest, but if he knew about Lionel Helswell he must have heard of the circumstances of his death.

Perhaps he anticipated some kind of pleasure from forcing her to tell him. If that was so, she was prepared to deny it to him.

Lightly, cynically, she replied, 'Yes. He got tied up in a financial scandal, used most of my mother's money and all of mine in an attempt to bail himself out, and when that had all gone put a gun in his mouth. Good job, too. He was a mean-minded martinet, and, like all bullies, fundamentally a coward. I don't miss him in the least.'

'Except that he dumped the responsibility for your mother on you. When did this happen?'

Aura shrugged. 'Six months ago.'

'Three months before you met Paul.'

Refusing to react to the steel in his words, she replied serenely, 'Yes, just before I met Paul.'

And he could make what he liked of that. She had already told him more than she had wanted to about her own life.

'Do *you* have relatives, or were you spat out of the ground, fully carved in stone?' she asked pertly.

He laughed. 'I have parents, and a variety of aunts and uncles and cousins.'

They talked a little about the Wairarapa; several of the girls Aura had been to school with came from there, and he knew their families. It was meaningless, harmless conversation. Keeping her eyes firmly fixed in front, she stared sightlessly as they made their way through suburbia towards the city, finally stopping under the wide *porte-cochère* of a hotel with a well-known and highly recommended restaurant on its top floor.

Flint had booked a table by the window so she was able to look out over the harbour, but Aura saw nothing beyond a blur of lights, the sheen of obsidian water, for her whole attention was taken by the man who walked beside her.

She had never experienced such utter absorption before, as though the only thing of any importance to her in the world was this man. She wanted to stop time, to hold back its inexorable flow and imprison the moment like a fly in amber, or the crystal brilliance at the heart of a diamond.

Yet beneath the mingled delight and pain lurked deep guilt. At last, with anger and despair, she accepted that she could not marry Paul. What had been unimaginable before was now the only honourable way to behave.

With that thought came the horrifyingly daunting prospect of cancelling the wedding.

The cruel, bitter irony of it all was that whatever she did she was doomed to loneliness. There was no future for her with Flint. She didn't trust him, she didn't like him; all she felt for him was a forbidden desire so potent that it overcame even love.

Because she did love Paul. That was what hurt so much.

The lamplight glittered on the diamond on her finger, transforming it to blue fire. Paul, she thought sadly, aware that even now she was thinking of him in the past, oh, Paul, my dearest, forgive me.

She looked up, to catch Flint's gaze, piercing, predatory, on her downcast face. A delicious shudder stabbed her spine, turned her bones to honey.

She began to talk with the sophisticated ease of a woman who knew her way around the world. Her *savoir-faire* was a shield, a thin, barely opaque barrier against those far too perceptive eyes, but it and pride was all she had for shelter.

Halfway through the delicious meal a caustic comment made by Flint about one of the other patrons surprised a catch of laughter from her. He surveyed her with gleaming eyes, his hard mouth curved, and she felt that look right down to her toes, felt it scorch a pattern through her that couldn't be erased.

Her heart leapt into feverish speed. The smile faded on her lips, an unruly hunger sharpened its claws on her body, and she was gripped by a need so acute, so frightening, that she lost colour. She had never known such passion, never understood how powerless reason and logic were against it.

Common sense told her that if she went ahead and married Paul she'd live a happy and fulfilled life. Paul loved her, and Flint manifestly didn't, yet all she wanted to do was follow him through whatever hells he might drag her. This 'dark, secret love' of Blake's poem was terrifying, but if he said *come*, she'd leave without a backward glance everything that had been so important to her and walk barefoot with him across the world.

Only he would never say that word. He saw her as someone with her eye to the main chance. Oh, he wanted her, but he was strong enough to deal with that. His sexuality wouldn't get in the way of his intelligence; that cold, clear incisive brain was completely in control of his hormones.

'What is it?' he asked.

Aura shrugged. 'A goose walked over my grave.' And added rapidly, 'So do you think we're really going to have power cuts until the southern lakes fill in the spring?' referring to the latest political scandal.

'It seems ominously like it,' he said. If he realised she was evading his question he chose not to probe, instead delivering an extremely trenchant criticism of those he considered had brought the country to this pass.

Playing devil's advocate, Aura made him justify every statement, and tried to enjoy the rest of the meal, acutely aware that remorse and apprehension dimmed her usual easy conversation. She was relieved when at last they were sitting in the seats Paul had chosen for her pleasure at the theatre.

Unfortunately, as the story of two friends as close as brothers who loved the same woman unfolded in front of her, she barely heard the ravishing music. At any other time she would have smiled at the weakness of the libretto. Now, it struck too near home.

Yet in spite of the emotions that churned through her, submerging her integrity in a dark tide of desire, she had never felt so vividly, achingly alive; it was as though all these years she had slept in a cocoon, watching the world but not part of it.

From the age of fourteen she had mistrusted men. Her assailant's spoken rape had corrupted her in ways she was only just beginning to understand, so that she had protected herself by freezing off her budding sexuality. That, and the misery of life with a mother too weak to protect her from a stepfather intent on breaking her spirit, had led to the two engagements Flint was so suspicious of. They had been escape bids.

Looking back, she could even work out why she had chosen each man. The first one, when she was barely eighteen, had happened a month after Alick and Laurel's first child was born. Her cousin had always been Aura's refuge, her anchor. The baby boy had signalled irrevocably that Alick's main loyalty now lay with Laurel and his new family. Aura had been once more relegated to the periphery.

And the second engagement had been a vain attempt to refute her first fiancé's accusations of frigidity.

Aura regretted both of them, because she had used both men, and hurt them.

After those fiascos she had refused to become serious with any man until Paul came along, the ideal, chivalrous hero of every virgin's dreams, offering protection and an unthreatening, unselfish love. Paul was safe. And

he understood. When she tried to tell him she was frigid
he had laughed softly.

'No one with your love of textures and colours and
perfumes, no one who uses their senses as you do, is
frigid,' he had said. 'You might have had bad experi-
ences in the past, but making love will come naturally
with you with the right man, a man you can trust.'

Then he'd kissed her, and she'd liked it, and because
he was so patently trustworthy she had learned to love
him.

He had been right. But it was Flint who had smashed
through her barriers. She didn't trust him as far as she
could throw him, but she wanted him with every sense
honed to a painful intensity.

He had ripped the shield of ice away, melted it in the
heat of his personality and exposed her unprotected, untried self to his potent, explicit masculinity.

By the time interval arrived she was tense and on edge,
so she drank the glass of white wine he bought her too
fast. Fortunately, friends and acquaintances kept her
answering questions about Paul's absence with what she
hoped was the correct mix of regret at his absence and
pleasure in Flint's company.

But she was almost convinced that everyone who
talked to her, looked at her, knew of her hypocrisy.

The second half was sheer hell. Aura tried to concentrate on the stage because it was easier than facing her
misery and self-reproach, but she couldn't take in what
was happening. Brilliantly clad people passed before her
vision, sang and postured, and she saw nothing because
her brain was feverishly sorting through alternatives.

She couldn't marry Paul feeling like this.

Yet this would die; something so intense couldn't last
for long. Paul was everything she wanted. It was aridly
ironic that in spite of the runaway fire Flint roused in
her, she didn't want to give up the security of Paul's love
for the doubtful bliss of an affair with Flint—even

supposing he wanted one. And the incident with Gemma made that highly unlikely. Loyalty, she thought agitatedly, was probably more important to him than satisfying a sexual need.

He wouldn't have any difficulty with that; she had only to glance around the foyer at interval to notice jealously the interested scrutiny he was getting from far too many women. His combination of raw sexuality and worldliness was overwhelming.

Aura's teeth sank into her lower lip, worrying the soft flesh. Exhausted, wracked by bitter pangs of conscience and equally bitter need, she asked herself why this had to happen to her. Just when she was getting her life together, when she could see some sort of peace and tranquillity ahead, she had to be dealt a wild card like Flint Jansen.

But that was self-pity; she had seen it render her mother ineffective too often to surrender to its power.

Like a force of nature, Flint had happened. And somehow she was going to have to deal with him and his effect on her life.

After the final curtain came down she stopped her polite applause and got to her feet, went out with him and into the car park. It was chilly; she shivered and instantly Flint switched on the heater. The motorway was surprisingly full of traffic, some of it erratic. Aura watched a car swerve in front of them without feeling any concern. Insulated from the world by her dilemma, she struggled to stay behind the façade of good manners.

Almost immediately the wayward car swung back into the next lane. Flint muttered something short and crisp, but his hands were steady on the wheel and he didn't show any outward sign of irritation.

'The driver must be drunk,' Aura said remotely.

'It certainly looks like it.' His voice was hard and unhurried.

The errant car wove its dangerous way through the traffic, then without warning shot over into their lane. Aura's hands covered her silent gasp. There was a terrifying squeal of brakes, the seatbelt tightened unbearably across her chest, and she heard her voice cry out Flint's name. Sparks flashed as the two vehicles collided in a nightmare of noise and motion, then the front car pulled away again, tearing off into the darkness.

'Are you all right?' Flint demanded in a voice she didn't recognise.

'Yes.' The whisper of sound alarmed her, so she repeated it more loudly. 'Yes, I'm perfectly all right.'

'I'll pull off and make sure we haven't done any severe damage to the car.'

Gritting her teeth, Aura wondered how on earth he could be so controlled, his hands so steady on the wheel.

'I got his number,' she said numbly, and quoted it before she forgot.

'Good girl.'

Such a tiny compliment, meaning nothing, yet the glow of his words affected every cell in her body.

Once they'd rolled to a stop on the verge he picked up a cell phone and dialled the emergency number, gave the number of the offending vehicle and his own name and address, and suggested crisply they get a traffic officer to intercept it quickly before the idiot killed himself or others.

The person at the other end said something. 'Oh, yes,' Flint replied in a voice as cold as ice, 'I'm more than happy to be a witness.'

Aura's skin prickled into a cold sweat. Putting the phone down, he commanded, 'Stay there,' before opening the door.

In the glare of the motorway lamps and the hard white headlights of the passing cars he looked harsh, like an ancient god of war, of strife and death, his features outlined strongly as he checked beneath the bonnet of the Jag.

When he returned Aura asked quietly, 'Anything wrong?'

'Nothing that I can see, but there's a strong smell of oil. I'm not going to drive the rest of the way to your place in case I've missed something. My flat's only a mile from here, so I'll take you there and ring a taxi to take you home.'

'I thought your flat was being decorated,' she said foolishly.

Sending a swift glance in her direction, he set the Jag in motion again. 'We won't be inside long enough for the smell of paint to worry us.'

He lived in the top floor of a big apartment building on the side of Mount Hobson, another of the small volcanoes that dotted the isthmus of Auckland. This building was not brashly modern like Paul's apartment block, and the security was unobtrusive. The porter looked up as they came in and nodded at them both, but beneath the respectful smile Aura was sure she detected a prurient interest. On the way up in the lift she shivered again, and once she had started she couldn't stop.

'Shock,' Flint said succinctly. 'I'll make some tea. You sit down and try to keep warm.'

Ignoring her protest, he stripped off his coat and dropped it around her shoulders. Warm and a little heavy, it smelt of his particular masculine essence. Rubbing her cheek for a guilty second against the collar, Aura watched as he moved about the luxurious kitchen with self-contained familiarity. He looked bigger in the stark white shirt than he had with the jacket on.

Her eyes lingered on the breadth of shoulder, the long arms, the way the muscles flexed as he leaned over to pour the hot water into the teapot.

Because this would probably be the only time she would ever be in his apartment, she dragged her gaze

away and tried to look around, but she was unable to
absorb anything beyond a dim impression of size and
spartan elegance. After a minute or so she gave up and
concentrated on stopping the tremors that racked her
body.

Counting as she took in even breaths failed dismally,
and she was beginning to wonder just what she had to
do to regain control when Flint emerged from the kitchen
with a mug of tea, only half full.

'Try this,' he said.

The hand she held out was shaking so much that she
stared at it in dismay.

He said, 'I'll hold it for you.'

She braced herself stiffly as he sat down beside her
on the sofa.

'I can't get it to your mouth if you turn your face
away,' he said, the amusement in his words making her
cringe.

Every instinct shouted at her to grab the mug herself,
but his lean fingers held it firmly, and she was not going
to indulge in an undignified wrestle for possession which
would proably spill the wretched stuff.

With a stubborn effort of will she turned her head and
let him hold the mug to her lips. The liquid within was
hot and milky and disgustingly sweet.

She must have pulled a face because he said instantly,
'I know it tastes foul but drink the lot, it will stop that
trembling.'

Her teeth chattered on the china.

He made an impatient sound, jerked the mug away
and put it on the table, then gathered her into his lap
like a baby, cradling her in his warm embrace. 'No, don't
move,' he said quietly. 'You just need a little reassuring.'

'I f-feel s-stupid,' she managed to say, but that wasn't
entirely what she meant. As well as weak and fragile,
she felt an overwhelming urge to give in, just lie in his
arms and let whatever was going to happen, happen.

'Why? It's a perfectly normal reaction to shock,' he said gravely, picking up the mug. Patiently, he held it to her lips until all the tea had gone.

'I'm s-sorry,' she muttered. 'It's so silly—I don't normally fall to bits like this.'

'You're in the habit of being clipped on the motorway?'

His voice sounded harsher, even a little grating. If she looked up she would see the angular line of his jaw.

Her smile was distorted into a grimace. 'N-no.' She drew a deep, jagged breath, trying to summon the energy to get up, move away.

Now that the sweet, hot tea was working its cure Aura was too aware of other things, the flexed muscles beneath her thighs, hard as a sheet of steel, the rise and fall of his chest against her shoulder, a faint masculine scent more erotic by far than the finest perfume. The steady, solid thud of his heart pulsed through her body, a primitive counterpoint to the skipping, thudding beat of her own. His heat encompassed her, at once comforting and a warning.

Aura was still trembling, but for a different reason. Needles of desire, sharp and pitiless, coalesced in the base of her stomach, were transformed by some mysterious sorcery into a fire that sprang fullblown to raging life. She was assailed by hunger, fierce, basic, not to be gainsaid; the moments when she had seen the other car hit them and wondered whether they were going to live or die had edged every emotion, sharpened sensation to a pitch that wouldn't be denied.

Yet deny it she must.

She said thinly, 'I'm all right, now, thank, you. I think you'd better ring for the taxi.'

'Certainly.'

But when she went to get up her legs didn't want to support her, and she had to clutch his shoulders to get her balance.

Startled, she looked down into eyes that were a continuation of the flames licking through her body, eyes that held a stark, heated promise, eyes that demanded and threatened her with pleasure untold.

She thought she whispered a denial, but if she did it was far too late and far too quiet, because he kissed her as though she was the gold at the end of his rainbow, the summit of all his ambitions.

His mouth was cruel, taking, not asking, and she could have fainted with the ecstasy of it. Yet the kiss frightened her, too, for it freed the wildness she had spent years trying to conquer and control, the wildness that urged her to yield, to follow where that kiss led, to grasp what it promised.

Temptation consumed her with its beckoning lure, tearing her apart. Aura had to resist it with every small bit of courage left.

She tried to push him away, but when her hands reached the collar of his shirt they curled around it, holding him close. Closing her eyes in surrender, she gave in to the demand that was eroding her will into nothingness.

After a moment his head lifted. Her lips were soft and red and throbbing, and they felt bereft.

Now, she told herself sturdily. Pull away, stand back, lift your head and let him see that you don't want any more...

'You kiss like a dream,' he said softly. 'But then, I knew you would. Your mouth is like a crushed rose, enigmatic yet sensual, hiding secrets and sweetness. I've wanted to kiss you ever since we met, when you looked at me with those hungry eyes, surprised yet expectant, as though you'd been waiting for me all your life.'

Shaking her head, Aura sprang free, backing away with her eyes fixed on his face. The scar stood out in bold prominence, thin and white against his bronzed skin.

'No.' But she stumbled over the word.

'Yes. You want me, Aura. Admit it.'

'No!'

Another step backwards, slow and secret, holding his fierce raptor's gaze with her own so he wouldn't notice her sly progress towards the safety of the door. Faced with such extreme danger she wasn't conscious of thinking; she reacted like a small animal in the presence of its greatest predator, doing what instinct bade her.

In a second she would turn and run for the door and the safety of the lift. He wouldn't chase her across the foyer with a porter on duty. Once outside, once free of the mindless enchantment that was scrambling her brain, she'd be safe.

He said roughly, 'Stop looking so terrified. I'm not going to hurt you.'

It seemed a good idea to acknowledge that. She nodded, and slid her other foot behind her.

Swift as a hawk striking death from the sky, moving with the lethal grace of a hunter, he was on his feet, and before she had time to turn he had caught her by the arm and swung her back, shaking her slightly.

'You're not running away from this,' he said calmly enough, but there was a ring of inexorable determination in his voice.

'Let me go!' she panted, trying to jerk her arm free.

His fingers tightened, and she cried out at the pain.

Swearing, he loosened them, but his free hand came up and caught her other arm so that she was held in a remorseless grip. Aura dragged air into tortured lungs, eyes measuring distances, measuring him.

She would have to knee him in the groin. She had never deliberately hurt anyone in her life, and she didn't think she could do it to him, but panic expanded inside her like a balloon, blocking out logic, blocking out everything but her knowledge that one kiss had changed everything.

Very quietly he warned, 'Try it, Aura, and you'll regret it more than you've ever regretted anything.'

She said desperately, 'Flint, I have to go home.'

'Not until you admit that you want me.'

'Go to hell,' she whispered, letting her lashes fall to hide her frantic gaze.

'Admit it, Aura. You want me to kiss you—that's what frightens you so much. You want to go to bed with me, lie with me in a tangle of sheets while we discover each other's mysteries, and then lose ourselves in them. *You want me*, Aura. Say it.'

Her pulse was rocketing into the stratosphere, his quick words summoning a white-hot response from deep within her, but although she had to dampen dry lips and swallow, she shook her head. If she once acknowledged his power she'd have no control over the rest of her life.

He laughed, and she thought she saw a flash of unwilling respect in the golden gaze. Then he pulled her close against the fierce heat of his body and kissed her again, a deep, deep kiss that probed past more than just the physical barriers of her resistance.

Aura tensed, but for the first time ever there was no faint niggle of disgust, no automatic rejection that had to be controlled before she could relax. Yet she would not give in.

Struggling, she turned her head from side to side, bit at him with small, sharp teeth. He laughed again, and bit her back, her lips and her cheek, under the fine line of her jaw, and down the sweet smoothness of her throat, little nips just short of pain that stimulated her unbearably.

The shock of strong teeth against her skin sapped Aura's resistance. She said something, words she didn't recognise escaped from her astonished mouth, and he lifted his head and kissed her again.

And she was lost.

CHAPTER FIVE

THIS was what she had longed for, this intimate mingling, the knowing, fierce exploration of her mouth, the sudden thrust that gave birth to racking shudders of sensation. Without volition her hands slid up, reached past shoulders as broad as the sky, to finally cling to his neck. He pulled her savagely into a body that was rigid with need.

Never before had Aura experienced such a feeling of rightness. She felt like the first woman, offering everything she was to the only man.

Flint wanted her. He couldn't hide that; he didn't even try. This man who could steal her soul with a kiss was as much at her mercy as she was at his. Stabbed by delight, by burgeoning rapture, she pressed against him, desperately trying to get closer to the male vigour and potency that had called to her from the moment she saw him.

He laughed deep in his throat. 'Yes, you like that, don't you. Do you like this?' as his hand slid around to cup the full curve of her breast.

Aura wavered, but the instantaneous excess of response as his thumb passed across a wildly sensitive nipple stopped the unborn protest.

'I see you do,' he said, and kissed her again, sealing her mouth as he carried her across the room to lower them both on to the long sofa, burying his face in her scented throat, his fingers working in the heavy mass of her hair to free it from confinement. As soon as the shining waves slithered across his wrist he lifted his head

97

and stared intently at the burgundy floss that clung like living silk to his fingers.

Fascinated, Aura watched him spread a wide swathe across her throat. He looked at her with fierce hunger in the glittering golden depths of his eyes.

'At first I thought you dyed it,' he said, his voice raw. 'It's like wine transformed into silk, fire rendered into solidity...' He teased the tress apart, then kissed her white throat through the licking, curling flames.

His words and the unexpected caress affected her unbearably. Shuddering, she whispered his name on an expelled breath, reacting helplessly when the contours of his face hardened even more, drew into lines of desire that should have terrified her.

But this was what she had been born for: to have Flint manoeuvre the fastening of her dress down and shape with gentle fingers the contours of her breast, the slightly rough tips of his fingers eliciting tremors that stoked up the inner heat at the junction of her body.

Lost in a sensual haze, abandoned by principles, by reason and logic, Aura touched her lips to his throat, licking the spot where his pulse throbbed. Instantly, his slow, seductive exploration stopped.

The harsh noise that erupted from deep in his chest brought her lashes up; she froze, but he said through clenched teeth, 'Go on.'

With wondering fingers she flicked the front of his shirt open and as her breath stopped in her lungs found the hot skin of his chest. Beneath the antique pattern of hair it was smooth and as fine-grained as satin.

Instinctively responding to a great surge of need, she tensed her muscles, arching her back. He cupped her breast, moulding it into the shape of his hand, and bent his head and kissed it, his mouth closing over the pleading peak.

Aura bucked with surprise and a fierce, untamed craving that whipped from the top of long-repressed desire like spindrift in a storm, carrying her with it. She groaned, the little sound guttural and surprising in the quiet room.

Beneath his tongue her nipples clamoured with a ruthless sensitivity that could only be soothed by his ministrations, yet the heat and moisture of his mouth did nothing but intensify it.

Aura didn't know when he slid her dress down so that her breasts were barely covered by the soft lace, she only knew that he was looking at her with such violent hunger that it summoned an answering depth of longing. Now she knew why people died for love, why kingdoms had fallen and governments toppled and lives been ruined by this savage delight.

He lifted his face. Almost all colour had been burned away in his eyes so that surrounding his enlarged pupils there was a rim of pure, blazing gold. Aflame in the dark fire of his gaze, she made no protest when he pulled her dress down to her waist and ripped his shirt open. Instead she went eagerly into an embrace as hard and final as fate, her breasts crushed by the hard wall of his chest. He kissed her, and she responded with the same fierce power, undulating her hips against the betraying rigidity that revealed he wanted her as much as she wanted him.

The pressure at once appeased and exacerbated her need. Winding her arms around him she pushed against him once more, rejoicing in the mounting thunder of his heart, yielding herself in a surrender she barely understood.

He turned, taking her with him, and in the same movement pushed the froth of lace dress all the way down, carrying her slip with it, so that all she had on was the black silk camisole and her garter belt and french knickers, and the black stockings that clad her long slender legs.

Aura's hands fluttered in an instinctive effort to cover herself.

'No,' he said thickly, his hand roving across the slightly curved surface of her stomach. His forefinger made a slow foray into the tight little indentation of her navel, and to her bewilderment that too was a pleasure point; his touch sent ripples of excitement through her.

'Did you think this might happen?' he asked, still in that same impeded voice. 'Did you dress for me tonight, Aura?'

Shivering, she tried to summon indignation as she shook her head, but his smile mocked her, and those tender, probing, inexorable fingers slid beneath the silk material of her knickers and touched her where she was moist and slick and hot, a mute, truthful capitulation, an appeal for something that had never happened before for her.

Aura shuddered, her back arcing helplessly as she closed her eyes, unable to meet the unchecked triumph in his face, the consummately male satisfaction that was echoed in his heavy-lidded gaze.

Rigors of sensation rushed through her; she was helpless before the smooth skill of his fingers, unable to resist, unable to want to. 'Flint,' she said weakly, on a sharply indrawn breath. 'Oh, God, Flint...'

'What do you want?' His voice was a low growl, the words indistinct. 'Tell me what you want, Aura, and I'll give it to you, I'll give you everything——'

The fire of his touch began to build, to drag her down in flame and thunder, to——

'Tell me now that you love Paul,' he said savagely as he got to his feet.

Paul. Oh, God, *Paul*!

Aura's hand flew up to cover her mouth. Huddling deep in the soft cushions of the sofa, she turned her head away from his unrelenting gaze.

Paul. She had forgotten Paul, forgotten everything in the sorcery of Flint's lovemaking. And she had stupidly thought that because she was enchanted, he would be, too.

But that fleeting glimpse of his face, its hard features clamped in contempt, showed her just how wrong she was. Anger, the bitter inhumanity of betrayal, welled up like black marsh water.

The wild passion of his lovemaking and her response had sliced through the chains forged by the years and her will around the tempestuous core of her personality, so it was the old Aura who retorted on a rising note of fury, 'I do love him, damn you to *hell*, you arrogant swine. This means nothing! *Nothing*!'

There was silence. Then, 'I wish I didn't believe you,' he said silkily.

His eyes were burning trails of ice over her face. Aura dragged a sobbing breath into painful lungs, and found some measure of control. Lethargically, she said, 'I don't expect you to understand.'

She turned her back and began scrambling back into her clothes. His harshly unamused laughter swept her head around.

'Do you understand yourself, Aura, or have you been so brainwashed by your parasite of a mother that you can't see beyond security?'

'I love him!'

His laughter was discordant, filled with a rage she understood because it burned within her, too. Long fingers on her shoulder turned her to face him.

'If you love him, why is your breath coming so quickly between your lips?' His thumb traced the line of her mouth, gentle yet inexorable. Fire seared through her.

'Why do you look at me with a famished desperation?' He kissed her eyelids closed. 'Why does that maddening little pulse beat faster than I can count in the ivory column of your throat? You want me, Aura.'

'It isn't love,' she said angrily, grabbing at her sanity.

'Who said anything about love? But if you feel like this about me, what sort of marriage are you going to have with Paul?'

His words beat at her like stones. If she let him see her defeat she was lost. She said mordantly, 'As good a marriage as I'm likely to have with anyone.'

'Do you really think he'd be satisfied with your sort of love? He's a man, Aura, a man with a man's needs, and the milk-and-water affection you've got to give him won't fulfil them. When he takes you into that bedroom on your honeymoon he won't accept meek resignation; he'll want a woman who meets his every approach with ardour and passion. Lying back on the sheets with resignation is going to infuriate him; he'll want you to touch him and kiss him, to open yourself to him and to explore his body with the same desire you've shown me, the same desire he is going to show.'

He looked down at her, contempt and something else turning his face to stone. 'I've seen him kiss you, remember,' he said uncompromisingly, 'seen you dance together, and it's more than plain that although he's panting with lust, you're not affected at all. You've got him so strung up with your virginal, touch-me-not air that he thinks it's going to be all right on the night, but it won't be, unless you're a far better actress than you've shown any signs of being. Because he'll want a response like the one I got from you. And you won't be able to give it. You'll have to act, and lie to him, just as you've been lying to him all along.'

Covering her face with her hands, Aura fought back nausea, and images that terrified her; images not of Paul, but of herself lying in a bed with the man who spoke so cruelly to her now, of his lean body poised to take and invade, of the contrast between her pale hands and his bronze skin as she discovered with loving subtlety all the manifold differences between man and woman.

Powerful and seductive, the images tugged at her heart, sent heat through her body, yet Flint had offered her nothing, not marriage, not even a love affair.

'Some sort of friend you are,' she said acidly.

His teeth showed in a bitter, unamused smile. 'Yeah. But eventually he'll thank me.'

'My mother used to tell me that, and I didn't believe her, either. You've got a nerve, abrogating his right to decide.'

He laughed and touched her cheek, his long fingers gentle yet commanding. Aura resisted, but without hurting her he turned her face so that she had to meet the blazing golden brilliance of his gaze. Even as she shut her eyes she knew it was too late; he had recognised her submission.

'You know you don't want to marry him,' he said crisply. 'Knights in shining armour are not for you, Aura. You don't need rescuing.'

'You're cruel,' she choked, torn in two by hate and desire.

He laughed again and his finger touched her mouth, sliding between her lips until she opened them. 'It takes a diamond to cut another diamond,' he said, stroking the wildly sensitive flesh of her upper lip in a whisper-soft enticement, then running his finger across the sharp cutting edge of her top teeth. 'You're cruel, too, cruel and imperious and vibrant with life, with your full, sulky red mouth and those witch's eyes, like jade sprinkled with gold. You want so much more than he can give you, you want everything that life offers. You won't get it with Paul.'

He put his finger into his mouth, tasting her, his narrowed gleaming eyes watching the way her breath hissed through her lips, the subtle droop of her lashes in unwilling response to the primitive little action.

'You don't know that,' she retorted, whipping up scorn because she was too close to surrendering.

He shrugged. 'I know Paul far better than you do. He's conventional and rather old-fashioned. Look at his mother; that's the sort of life he sees you leading. He'll keep you chained by love until it turns into dissatisfaction and despair, and then into hatred...'

'Not Paul,' she retorted.

'You're nothing but a leech,' he snarled, suddenly furious. 'At first I thought it was the money, but it's not entirely that, is it, although the money's important.'

White-faced, her eyes gleaming with supressed tears, she spat, 'I am not marrying Paul for his money!'

He surprised her by nodding, his gaze never leaving her face. He was pale too, and the scar stood out lividly on his cheek, ending in a devilish flick along the unyielding line of his jaw.

'Not entirely, perhaps. You want his strength and his stability, you want to use him as a shelter from the world, make him take the place of your father and your cousin. Nice, safe relationships, both of them, except that your father left you, and so did Alick in a different way. He got married. You had no one to rely on then, so you went looking for someone who would take care of you.'

'No!'

'Oh, yes. Your stepfather killed himself—another man who left you, but this time he left you with a silly, flirting, useless mother on your hands.'

'You are foul,' she shouted, losing control entirely. 'I did not "go looking"!' She mimicked his tone, mocking him with angrily sparking eyes and contemptuous mouth.

His smile was cool and aggravating. 'I don't blame you, not entirely. You've been well conditioned. Your mother found men she could lean on, so you followed her footsteps and conveniently fell in love with Paul. Of course, he wants you to depend on him because that way he can pretend to be the stronger. But his sort of strength is not what you need. If you marry him, in five years' time you'll be bored stiff and giving him hell.'

'Whereas you're strong, I suppose,' she jeered.

'I'm strong,' he agreed, a simple statement of fact by a man who knew himself so well he didn't need to boast. 'But don't think you're going to change one support for another. I'm not offering you anything, Aura, not a shoulder, not a shelter in bad weather, not anything. You're not going to be able to say that I seduced you. When you come to me you'll be free, and you'll understand exactly what you're doing.'

He spoke with a callous detachment that shattered the last shreds of her composure. 'I want to go home!' she said raggedly into the aching silence.

'The taxi must be here by now. Just remember one thing.' His voice hardened, became merciless and unsparing. 'Sooner or later, whether you marry Paul or not, you and I are going to make love. Ask yourself which will hurt him most.'

It wasn't a threat, it was a straight promise. With the implacable words ringing in her ears, echoing through her soul, Aura swung on her heel.

'All this,' she said in her haughtiest voice, 'because I refuse to go to bed with you.'

The instant the words left her tongue she saw them strike home. His smile was devilish, his pitiless eyes lit from within by the fires of hell as with calculated slowness he pulled her into him, letting her feel the merciless, naked force of his sensuality, and the aggression bound up with it.

She fought, but he was too strong. Not that he hurt her; with insulting ease he let her tire herself out. He was aroused, but instead of the involuntary withdrawal she felt in Paul's arms she was almost suffocated by a ferocious exultation.

It was this which made her mind up. She lifted her flushed, passionate face and said between her teeth, 'If you do anything more I'll sue you for assault and attempted rape.'

He laughed, his breath soft and heated across her incredibly tender mouth. 'And I'll countersue,' he mocked. 'You can't marry him, Aura.'

She knew that, but if she said so she would have no protection against the desire that beat through her, linking them in a conflagration strong enough to destroy everything she had ever learned in her life and set her adrift on a sea that was unknown and more perilous than any other.

Closing her eyes against the command in his, she fixed her jaw, set her mouth into a mulish line. 'I'll do what is best for me,' she said thinly. 'I'm no foolish girl, to be seduced out of my mind.'

'No, you're not. That ripe beauty hides a tough little adventuress, determined to keep on a course that you must know will short-change Paul, even if he never learns that you don't love him.'

'I do love him!' she swore.

'So you're going to go through with it?'

Jerking herself free, she spoke as calmly, as steadily as she could. 'It isn't anything to do with you, Flint. I'm going home. *Now*.'

His bluntly chiselled face was unmoving, no emotion but residual passion flickering in the depths of his eyes, yet Aura sensed that at that moment she was in greater danger than she had ever been in her life.

Then, to her astonishment, he laughed. 'All right,' he said, and took her down to the foyer and put her in the taxi, saying with sardonic amusement, 'Thank you for a very interesting evening, Aura.'

Fury contested with chagrin and a grief so deep she refused to acknowledge it. Staring straight ahead she said tonelessly, 'Goodnight.'

By the time she reached home, however, the fury had died and the wilderness of ardour had been swamped by shame; she was left with the bitter taste of gall in her mouth.

All of her rationalisations were revealed for what they were: specious and self-serving. Flint was right. What she felt for Paul had nothing of the fiery inevitability, the rightness she felt in Flint's arms.

And because of that, she couldn't marry Paul, even though she loved him. She walked slowly up the path towards the front door, twisting Paul's diamond on her finger, watching the cold light of the moon sparkle within its heart. The starry pink and white flowers of jasmine glimmered in the darkness, their musky, potent scent floating sweetly on the fresh, crisp air.

She rubbed her cold arms, listening to a siren wobbling along the motorway, spreading fear and desolation. An ambulance; she spared a thought for the person it carried, or was heading towards.

She didn't want to be here. She wanted to be in the country somewhere, where the only night noises were pleasant, unthreatening rural ones, dogs howling a lullaby to the moon, moreporks calling wistfully from the bush, the soft liquid chuckle of a stream running through paddocks.

It was utter cowardice, of course. She just wanted to run away from the mess her life had suddenly become. Only there was no one else to deal with it. It was her mess, and she was going to have to clean it up as best she could.

When Paul came back from Samoa she'd have to tell him that she couldn't marry him. After that, it would be Natalie's turn. All the people they had invited to the wedding, as well as the florist and the caterer and a dozen others, would have to be told. The presents would have to be sent back. And she'd have to do it all, because Natalie wouldn't be able to.

Her heart quailed. It was going to be awful, and the years that followed would be awful too, with her mother constantly casting it up at her that she had whistled away security for them both on a whim. Natalie would never

do such a thing. And Aura wasn't going to be able to
tell anyone, much less Paul, why she had changed her
mind.

Flint had made it obvious that he didn't see any sort
of future for them together. She couldn't hurt Paul even
more by telling him that she had fallen in lust with his
best friend.

Because that was all it was. She had no illusions about
that. Love implied shared interests, shared commit-
ments. She had that with Paul. This overwhelming
hunger that had her caught fast in its thrall was superficial, a thing of dazzle and flash with no substance to
it. She and Flint shared nothing except a flaming attraction which would peter away in time. That time
couldn't come too soon for her.

Aura had always thought that it was mainly men who
were able to separate their emotional lives, loving in one
compartment, lusting in another, and no communi-
cation between the two. Perhaps there was something
wrong with her.

Or perhaps, she thought, unlocking the door, it was
just bad luck, like being caught in an earthquake or a
tidal wave. Flint had had much the same effect on her
life as a natural disaster.

When she woke after another almost sleepless night it
was to hear Alick's voice outside.

A moment later there was a tap at the window. 'Are
you awake?' he asked.

Aura groaned. 'Just. Wait a minute.'

By the time she opened the door Laurel was standing
there while Alick appeared to be examining the con-
nection where the power line went into the unit.

'He thinks it looks a bit wonky,' Laurel explained.

Aura liked Alick's wife very much, but at that moment
she didn't want to have to meet her too perceptive,
golden-brown eyes.

'We thought you might like to have a quiet day with us,' she went on, eyeing Aura with exactly the shrewd glance she dreaded. 'Actually, it will be with Alick. I'm spending the rest of the day with my mother, but Alick says it's months since he had a cousinly chat with you.' She followed Aura into the room and closed the door behind her, confiding with a twinkle, 'I think he's rather jealous. He's always had a special feeling for you, and now that you're going to get married—what's the matter?'

Aura shook her head, but Laurel's slim figure wavered through the tears in her eyes. Laurel looped her arms around her. 'I don't know anyone I'd rather confide in than Alick,' she said, holding Aura gently.

After an inelegant sniff Aura said on a wobble, 'No, I don't either.'

Laurel squeezed her then let her go with a little push towards the bedroom. 'So put some clothes on.'

Obediently, Aura dressed, went in to tell her mother what she was doing, and left.

Because this was a flying visit, the children, two sons and a charming, self-possessed three-year-old called Miriel who was Aura's goddaughter, had been left at Kerikeri. The apartment seemed empty without their voices, like little birds, in every room. Within a few minutes of their arrival Laurel left them.

It was a superb day, blue and gold and green, so fresh and clear that it tasted like wine on the tongue.

'Let's go out on to the terrace,' Aura said. 'How's the weather at Kerikeri? It's been just awful here, rain and more rain and winds from every point of the compass but mostly from the south and west, and bitterly cold.'

The sun lapped her in a tide of warmth. Still babbling about the weather, she collapsed on to a lounger.

'All right, young Aura,' Alick interrupted calmly, 'what's the matter?'

Her lips trembled. It would have been altogether too easy to fling herself on him as she used to when she was sixteen, but this was something that even the kindest of cousins couldn't help her with. Resolutely keeping her face turned away, she shook her head.

'Sometimes,' he said dispassionately, 'it can help to talk things over with a more or less impartial observer.'

She had taken her woes and fears to him for so long that it had become a habit, one she had tried to break. Was Flint right? Had she become accustomed to looking for support?

'Come on, Aura,' Alick said insistently. 'Spill.'

She surrendered. 'I can't marry Paul,' she said baldly.

He nodded. 'Flint, is it?'

'Is it so obvious?' she blurted. Would Paul realise who it was?

'Not to anyone else, I imagine, but I've known you far longer than most people.'

She bit her lip against an onslaught of tears. He waited silently until she regained enough composure to speak. 'The awful thing is that I don't love Flint. I mean—I don't know him. I do love Paul, so much, he's every-thing I want in a man, and I can't bear to hurt him, but——' she clenched her hands, forcing the words out for the first time '—I don't want to go to bed with him.'

'And you do want to go to bed with Flint.'

Alick's voice was without censure, but Aura nodded in shame. 'Yes,' she whispered.

'Do you remember Jenna? I was engaged to her when I met Laurel.'

Aura had forgotten. Alick and his wife were so ideal a couple, so much in love, that the girl he had chosen **first** had faded into the past. 'Jenna,' she said after a moment. 'Yes, I remember her. She was nice, but very young.'

'At the time she was exactly what I thought I wanted. But I knew the minute I met Laurel that it wasn't going to work.'

'Yes, but Laurel was in love with you,' she said wearily. 'I remember; it was obvious right from the start. Flint is not in the least in love with me. He's made that quite plain.'

'Has he? That doesn't really matter. What does matter is that you can't marry Paul McAlpine feeling the way you do about Jansen.'

It seemed so easy, stated in Alick's calm voice. Aura gulped and nodded. 'I know.'

'So what are you going to do about it?'

Wretchedly, Aura sighed. 'I'll have to tell Paul. He's in Samoa, and won't be back until Tuesday. Then it will be Natalie.'

'You can leave her to me,' he said cynically.

She sat with her head bent, pleating the folds of her skirt between fingers that trembled. 'It's not so simple,' she muttered. 'Paul's buying a flat for Mother—she'll be so angry, so upset.'

'Come on now, Aura, you know better than that! Your mother made a mess of her life. There's no need to make a mess of yours as well just to keep her in clover.'

'Paul will be hurt.'

He said remorselessly, 'Jenna was hurt when I broke it off with her. I don't know what's going to happen between you and Flint, whether he's just an excuse because in your inner heart you know that marrying Paul is wrong, but the point is that you don't want to marry Paul.'

Her teeth clamped down on her lips so hard she could taste the blood. 'But I do,' she wailed.

'Really? Then what's all this about?'

'Oh, *hell*.'

'Face facts, Aura.'

'I hate people who tell me to face facts,' she shouted, thumping her clenched fist on the arm of the lounger.

'That's Natalie speaking, not you. It's not going to be fun,' he admitted with wry humour, 'but Laurel and I will help as much as we can.'

For a moment she was tempted. 'No, I got myself into this,' she said huskily, 'I'll deal with it.'

The sun was setting smokily and dramatically behind a bank of clouds when she arrived back home in a far more stable frame of mind. Unfortunately, it was short-lived.

When she walked through the door her mother leapt to her feet, and in her surprise dropped a piece of paper.

'I'll get it,' Aura said, automatically reaching down to pick it up.

'No, no, it's all right.' Natalie's voice was even more betraying than the speed with which she snatched the paper away.

But Aura had recognised the heading. She asked in a ghost voice, 'How much do you owe on your credit card?'

Natalie's hand shook. 'Only a few thousand,' she said unsteadily.

'A few thousand?' Aura took advantage of her mother's shock to wrest the account from her. She looked down, and felt the colour run from her skin, leaving her cold and disorientated. 'That's more than a few thousand dollars.'

'Yes, well, how do you think I've been able to keep going?' Her mother was angry now, her usual tactic when confronted with money.

Tears next, Aura thought, fighting a bewildering sense of disconnectedness.

Sure enough, Natalie's eyes misted delicately. 'It's all right,' she said placatingly. 'I'll be able to pay for it as soon as you get married.'

'What do you mean?' Aura's voice was constricted, the emotion so tightly restrained it sounded harsh.

'Well, when I move into the new apartment I can sell this one, and pay the bill.'

Aura sat down, holding herself very stiff while she strove to assimilate this new blow.

If she didn't marry Paul there was no way she or her mother could pay the bill.

She said dully, 'What on earth did you spend it on?'

'I had debts when Lionel died—he wouldn't give me any money for a year or so. I had to pay for the funeral, and then—I had to get a dress made for the wedding. Well, I can't wear just any old rag, can I...' Natalie gestured vaguely, before beginning to weep in real earnest.

'It's all right,' Aura said tonelessly. 'Don't cry. We'll manage.'

'Of course we'll manage,' Natalie said, patting her eyes with a tiny, lacy handkerchief. She held out her hand for the bill, and spent the rest of the evening resolutely ignoring it and her daughter.

Who was racked by an inner torment she couldn't let her mother see. Inactivity fretted her nerves to shreds, for of course she couldn't do anything until she had told Paul. Unable to sleep again that night, she greeted the new week with resignation. She had clung to her great-grandmother's garnets through everything else, but now they would have to go. And even though they were the much rarer and more valuable green stones, they were not going to sell for anything like the amount Natalie owed.

A visit to the firm of jewellers who had sold her great-grandfather the garnets so many years before confirmed her fears. Dry-eyed, she handed them over, got the cheque, and paid it into Natalie's credit card account.

On her way back home, she sat slumped in the bus, trying to work out ways of getting the rest of the money.

Her computer set-up wouldn't bring much in, but it might buy time. They would have to mortgage the flat. I had better, she thought grimly, make sure Mother hasn't already done that.

She came home to find Natalie staring at a heap of presents that had arrived by courier. She looked sideways at Aura, then said quickly, 'Oh, good, you're back in time.'

'In time for what?'

Her mother laughed. 'Oh, in time for you to take these over to Paul's.'

'I'll take them over later,' Aura said vaguely. 'Tomorrow.'

'Oh, take them now. You know they clutter up this place far too much. Get a taxi, there's a good girl, and drop that pile off. Didn't I see another registered parcel card in the mail?'

'Yes.'

'Then you'd better collect it, too, hadn't you?'

There was no way Aura was going to be able to carry the boxes to the nearest bus stop. What the hell, she thought numbly. She had just enough money to pay for a taxi. So she rang one, and when it arrived piled the gifts into it and directed him to the post office. She collected the registered one and put it into the cab, when a sudden idea came to her.

'Wait a moment,' she said, and dashed across the pavement to the phone box. She dialled Paul's number, then stood with white knuckles waiting for someone to answer the call.

No one did, so Flint wasn't there. No, of course he wouldn't be, he'd be at work. If he had any decency at all, she thought savagely as she got back into the cab and gave Paul's address, he'd have moved back to his own apartment.

But his presence was stamped all over the flat. The morning's newspaper lay folded on a table, a rinsed coffee-mug sat upturned on the bench, and a silk tie that didn't belong to Paul had been slung across the back of the sofa.

Her stomach lurched. Setting her mouth into a thin line, she took the parcels into the spare room they had set aside for gifts.

Once they were safely stowed she stood for a moment staring around at the array. There were some lovely things there, chosen with love and care, objects she had looked forward to seeing in her home. Sudden tears stung her eyes unbearably.

She had almost reached the door when it was pushed open. The blood drained from her skin as Flint's tall, lithe form strode through, blocking the light from the landing.

Unable to speak, she stopped abruptly. His eyes raked her pale face, came to rest for a wildly unsettling moment on her mouth, then moved to hold her appalled gaze.

'You look like death,' he said.

'Thanks. What are you doing here?'

Almost absently he said, 'Organising myself out of here and into my own place.'

Aura bit her lip. The silence was so oppressive that she gabbled, 'I've just put some wedding-gifts in—in the room.'

His mouth hardened. There was a moment of taut silence before he said levelly, 'I see. So greed overcame integrity. But perhaps you didn't have much integrity to begin with.'

Anger burned deep and revivifying beneath the shock and the pain. He jumped to conclusions far too fast. 'Whatever I do, it's none of your concern,' she snapped back. 'Mind your own business, will you?'

'Just tell me,' he commented. 'Are you planning to go ahead with it?'

She lifted her head arrogantly. 'I've already told you what I'll do. I'll do what's right for me.'

He said something between his teeth, something she was rather glad she didn't hear, then snarled, 'Like hell you will! What got to you? Has Natalie sung a sad story about how awful it is to be poor, perhaps? Or did you decide that so many women down the centuries have gritted their teeth and counted their bank balances whenever their husbands touched them that it must be easy to do?'

'You make me sick,' she said frigidly, turning to walk past him and out of the door.

He grabbed her arm. 'That's nothing to what you do to me, Aura——'

'Let me go!'

He exerted some of his strength. Not enough to hurt her, but more than enough to pull her inexorably close to him.

She said icily, 'Take your hands off me, you coward.'

His eyes had narrowed into golden slits, but at that they opened, and it was like looking into the pits of hell. 'That's a funny word for you to use,' he said offensively, his breath stirring the strands of hair across her forehead. 'You're a lying, betraying bitch, a cold little whore with her eyes firmly fixed on the main chance, yet you call me a——'

Stung, as angry as he was, she spat, 'Yet in spite of all that you want me! So what does that make you, Flint?'

'A fool,' he said, his lips barely moving. He lifted his free hand and ran a long finger from one side of her jawbone to the other, tilting her face to meet his merciless scrutiny.

It was like being hit with a cattle prod; a violent shock of electricity sizzled through her, arching her body into the warmth and heat of his. Aura tried to wrench herself away, but his hand on her arm kept her close. Something ugly and violent moved in the glittering depths behind his thick, straight lashes.

'Yes,' he said, cupping her jaw, stroking up towards her ear, toying with the small sensitive lobe.

The breath stopped in Aura's throat. She had never thought of her ear as an erogenous zone, never realised that it could send such intensely erotic messages to the rest of her body. She stood with wide, dazed eyes while the small caress seared through her inhibitions and the fragile bonds of her honour.

'You have an amazing air of innocence, as though everything we do is fresh and new to you,' he said softly, watching her with a cold smile barely curving his hard mouth. 'Does it surprise you when you enjoy a man's touch, Aura? Hasn't any other man made you burn like this?'

Her throat was dry; she couldn't have spoken even if she had found words to say. His finger moved, slid into the sensitive inner reaches of her ear, and she shivered, mutely begging him to stop, to let her go.

'I wonder why?' he said in that gravelly voice. 'Was it because you chose them for their money?'

Trying to hide from the mesmerising spell of his gaze, to free herself of the boneless lethargy that had swept over her at his touch, she closed her heavy lids.

Abruptly he let her go. 'Do you want me to tell him?'

For a moment she was tempted, but almost immediately shook her head. She couldn't take the coward's way out.

'Tell him as soon as he gets home,' he ordered, looking at his watch. 'Or I'll do it for you.'

Aura looked at him with astonishment and anger in her heart. He had manipulated her, once more. Thank God, she thought defiantly, she didn't love him. But oh, when he touched her, her body knew its master.

Then Paul said from the doorway, 'What the hell is going on here?'

Shame flooded Aura in chilling waves, cutting the ground from beneath her feet. The face she turned to

the door was slack-jawed in shock, her crimson cheeks
and drowsy eyes giving her away completely.

She couldn't think of anything to say, anything to do,
except stare at a man she had never known existed. Her
gentle Paul was gone and in his place there was a hard-
faced stranger.

He knew, she thought, panic-stricken as she realised
that he had seen her in Flint's arms.

'What do you think?' Flint asked harshly, looking at
his friend with cold speculation.

'It looks as though I should have been protecting my
interests.' Paul's pleasant voice was icy. 'How long has
this been going on?'

'Nothing's been going on,' Aura said quickly, but her
face and tone gave her away.

'Don't lie to me,' he said wearily. 'For God's sake,
Aura, don't lie! What I saw a moment ago
wasn't——' He closed his eyes a second, then forced
them open. He looked only at her, not at the man who
stood beside her with the watchful, alert patience of a
tiger ready to make a kill. 'It wasn't what Flint said, or
even the way he touched you, it was the—how long has
it been going on?'

Aura took a deep breath, her eyes filling with useless
tears as they searched his beloved face.

'Since I saw her,' Flint told him, his face implacable.

'No,' Aura whispered hopelessly.

He looked at her with something like contempt. 'Yes.'

'Have you slept together?'

The question came toneless and fast. Aura looked at
the man she was still engaged to and saw fists clench.
'No!' The word burst from her lips, but Flint's abrasive
voice overrode hers.

'What do you think?' he asked again. This time there
was a note of insolence in the question, as though he
wanted to provoke Paul.

Anger and a corroding bitterness darkened Paul's face. 'You've never let friendship stand in the way of a woman you wanted, have you, Flint?' he said, the white line around his lips belying his calmness. 'Get out, both of you.'

'Paul——'

The imperative summons of a beeper interrupted, but Aura scarcely heard it. When she said his name again, he didn't even look at her, merely repeated indifferently, 'Get out.'

Amazingly, Flint reached over and grabbed a telephone, beginning to punch in numbers. Equally amazingly, Paul didn't try to stop him.

Aura turned away, her dreams shattering on the floor behind her. The sound of Flint's voice barking orders into the telephone was the last thing she heard as she closed the door behind her and walked out, away from the happy life she had so longed for, out into a darkness and cold nowhere as extreme as the desolation in her heart.

It was raining, but she didn't notice, bent only on reaching the sanctuary of home. She didn't think about the scene she had just endured; once she began she wouldn't be able to control herself, and it would be too humiliating to walk the three miles home weeping.

In the end that was what she did, rain mingling with the tears and washing them away in a chilly flood. Fortunately Natalie wasn't there. Still offended, she had decided to dine with friends a little out of town; if the weather worsened she intended to stay the night. Aura prayed that she would.

After she had showered and changed into old jeans and a jersey, she sat down with her notebook in front of her and began methodically to call every guest, every firm, to tell them that the wedding was cancelled.

Two hours later she put the receiver down, exhausted, feeling as though she had been beaten with a stick. Tears trickled down her cheeks; she bent her head and wept for everything she had thrown away because of bondage to a man who didn't love her, a man she didn't love.

The knock on the door made her freeze with sheer terror; she couldn't let anyone see her like this. As she tried to stop the sobs that forced themselves upwards, she crouched like a threatened wild animal into the chair.

'I know you're there.' Flint's voice, commanding and abrupt. 'Let me in, Aura.'

A tiny flame of hope, wavering in the winds of uncertainty, sprang to life inside her. Wiping her eyes, she walked across to open the door.

He looked big and vital and braced against some undefined tension, his harshly-contoured face and dark hair sprinkled with raindrops. The hand over her heart clenched tightly as she let herself recall the honeyed tide of desire his touch aroused.

'Crying?' His gaze travelled from her red eyes to her quivering lips. Some swiftly hidden emotion darkened the pure golden depths beneath his lashes. 'It's a waste of time. You certainly don't look as though it's doing you any good.'

'You're so kind,' she said, swallowing so that her voice was firmer. 'What do you want?'

'I want you to promise that even if he wants you to, you won't see Paul alone.'

CHAPTER SIX

AURA stared silently at him as the fragile flicker of hope died.

Impatiently he said, 'He's not reacting well to this.'

'Did you expect him to?' she asked in a voice whose bitterness was at her own folly.

'That doesn't matter. You are not to see him unless Natalie or someone else is with you, understand?'

Her mouth opened to tell him to go to hell when the beeper burst into life once more. He muttered a curse, then demanded, 'May I use your telephone?'

'Yes, of course.' Not that her permission was necessary; he was already halfway across the room.

It was a short conversation. He said, 'Yes, yes, yes. All right, just make sure that no one goes anywhere near the place or I'll deal with them myself. How the hell do I know, you're the man on the spot! Fob them off as best you can until I get there,' and hung up. 'I have to go,' he said, turning to meet her bewildered eyes. 'I'm due at the airport now. Aura, just promise me, please.'

'All right, I promise. Where are you going?' A confusion of emotions drained Aura's voice of all expression. Overriding her bleak acceptance of his departure was a sudden foreboding.

His features tightened. 'It doesn't matter.'

The foreboding became fear. She looked at him with eyes that took in everything, the striking features, the arrogantly outlined mouth, the scar, mute witness to some situation he hadn't been able to handle. Although the fact that he had survived presumably meant that he had dealt with it successfully.

'Take care,' she said, hardly able to articulate the words.

He hesitated, then swung towards her and kissed her as though she was all that he had ever wanted, as though he was famished for her and would never kiss her again.

Aura gave herself wholly to him, moulding herself to the lean strength of his big body.

'Goodbye,' he said huskily, and was gone, striding through the rain to where a long, blue car waited. As soon as its door swung closed behind him the vehicle purred off into the rapidly thickening afternoon.

Aura walked across to the kitchen and automatically put the kettle on. When she had made tea she had sat down and attempted to formulate a plan of action.

But her mind kept slipping back to the scene in Paul's apartment. How strange that he had turned up at that particular moment, when he wasn't due back until tomorrow. Her mind worried at the strangeness, until a faint niggling suspicion, a hint of unease, shreds and patches of information fed into her brain by barely understood mechanisms, consolidated into the conviction that Flint had known Paul was arriving home early. That was why he'd turned up. Not to collect his gear and go back to his own flat; no, he'd come for the express purpose of forcing the issue.

How had he known she would be there?

That was easy. Natalie, of course. She had almost pushed Aura out of the door with those parcels. What story had Flint spun to persuade her to make sure Aura was there at a certain time?

Flint had looked at his watch in the apartment as though wondering how much longer Paul was going to be.

Yes, that was typical of Flint. He was accustomed to being the man in charge, the man who took control and fixed things. It would be like him to engineer a confrontation.

With conviction came a cold, hard anger, sweeping away the dull lethargy that had pitched her into despair. Drinking her tea, she began to make lists. Being busy would keep the pain and the remorse at bay for a few days, although eventually she would have to deal with them.

But her hands shook slightly, and the skin was clammy. 'It's because I'm cold,' she said aloud, and got up.

The power shortage had persuaded her to use the heater as little as possible, and most days she didn't put it on until after dark, but the black clouds were being chased across the sky by a brisk sou'-westerly, and the temperature had dropped.

God, she thought wearily, will this winter never end?

The days that followed were sheer hell.

First of all she had to cope with Natalie, who ranted and wept and accused her furiously of ruining her life. Questioning that rapidly degenerated into a shouting match elicited, just as Aura dreaded, that her mother had mortgaged the unit to buy back some of her old furniture for the new apartment. With splendid disregard for actual value, she had contacted the new owners and offered them whatever was needed to persuade them to sell.

The furniture was being held in store; the business of organising its sale took up time and effort that Aura could ill afford, and because it had to be auctioned, no money came in to help pay back the mortgage.

As it was, the agent she dealt with told her that she wasn't likely to get much more than half of the amount her mother had paid for it. Natalie was no help; once more she retired to her bed, refusing to eat or get up.

The sheer logistics of cancelling the wedding exhausted Aura. Alick and Laurel helped, but she insisted on doing the brunt of the work.

'You're punishing yourself,' Laurel said astutely.

Aura shrugged. 'It stops me thinking.'

She heard nothing from Paul apart from an impersonal note informing her that the engagement ring had arrived safely. There was one very sticky telephone call from his mother. Laurel, bless her, had met Mrs McAlpine and they had agreed that she should deal with the presents from their side of the family.

'How is Paul?' Aura asked his mother tentatively.

'Broken-hearted. How did you expect him to be?'

Aura had always known that his mother didn't like her, but she was shocked by the venom that showed through the crisp tones. 'I'm sorry,' she said.

'I'm sure you will be, when you realise what you've done. Just as I'm sure Paul will come to his senses and see how disastrous a marriage between you would have been.'

'No doubt he will,' Aura said quietly, 'in which case both of you will perhaps feel some sort of gratitude to me. After all, a broken engagement is bad enough, but a broken marriage is much worse. Goodbye, Mrs McAlpine. Thank you for all you've done for me.'

Jessica, too, was a great help whenever she could get time away from the agency. It was she who told Aura that Paul had gone abroad.

'Big-game hunting in Africa, I suppose,' Aura said acidly. Trust a man to run away and leave the women to deal with everything.

Jessica didn't catch the allusion. 'No, he's gone climbing mountains in Nepal, so Mrs McAlpine told Mother. I can just see Paul up a mountain, somehow, can't you? He should be at home among the glaciers. How are you?'

Like everyone else, Jessica was dying to know who had broken the engagement and why, but, also like everyone else, she didn't ask.

'I'm fine,' Aura lied, collapsing bonelessly on to the sofa.

The days had dragged by without a word from Flint. Not that she'd expected him to contact her, but this casual underlining of how little she meant to him hurt.

She straightened up. 'I've done everything that needs to be done. I hope. Now I just want to crawl away and die somewhere.'

'Not you, you've got too much spirit for that. How's your mother?'

Aura cast a harried look towards the bedroom door. 'Not well,' she admitted.

Jessica grimaced, then asked, 'What are you going to do?'

'I'm going to find a job,' Aura told her.

'Doing what?'

Aura shrugged. 'Doing anything that gets me a hell of a lot of money.'

To her horror the tears she had been able to hold back until then flooded her eyes. She sniffed, but they continued to fall.

'What's she done now?' Jessica asked in an outraged voice, hugging her close as she stuffed a wad of tissues into her hand.

In as few words as possible, Aura told her

Jessica said on an appalled note, 'Your great-grandmother's garnets? Oh, Aura——'

'Yes, but they weren't enough. Not nearly enough.'

'So you need money, and you need it fast. Can't you borrow it against the value of this unit? Just temporarily? Because that software thingy you've been working on is going to sell for megabucks when you finish it.'

'If I ever do. I had to sell the computer, too. And the unit's no good. It's mortgaged.'

Jessica looked her horror. 'How's she going to make the payments?'

'She can't.' Aura drew in a shaking breath and firmed her voice. 'Neither can I. If I could get an uninterrupted

three months I could finish the marketing research programme. I'd have to hire a computer, of course.'

'And of course you can't get an uninterrupted three
months, either.'

'No, and even if I do, it's not going to mean instant
money, and that, Jess, is what I need. Because if I don't
get it, I can't pay the interest, let alone any principal,
on the loan. And you know what that means. This place
will be sold over our heads.'

Jessica snorted. 'Even if you do get some money or
a job, what about your mother then? Is she going to be
able to cope, or are you going to be mortgaging your
life to bale her out, time and time again?'

Aura's mouth tightened. 'She'll just have to learn to
live within her income. Damn it, Jess, it's not as though
she's poverty-stricken. She has a small income—bloody
Lionel couldn't dip his sticky fingers into her trust. My
grandfather set it up too tightly. The only reason he got
into mine was because she and my father were trustees,
and she signed everything over to Lionel when she
married him. She should be able to manage!'

'Yes, but she's never had to watch her spending.'

'Oh, damn my grandfather.'

'You can't blame him entirely,' Jessica pointed out,
exasperation vying with a need to be fair. 'He may have
started her off wrong, but she's had a good few years
to grow up. She didn't *have* to let Lionel run through
everything you both had. She could have taken some
interest in her own affairs.'

Aura sighed and frowned and rubbed her forehead.
'I know. She's just going to have to learn how to deal
with life.'

Jessica looked at her keenly. 'It's about time.
You've played nursemaid for long enough. Look, I
might be able to do something about this. I can't
promise anything——'

'I'm too short to be a model,' Aura said, blowing her nose with vigour and feeling oddly better.

'Yes, but you've got fabulous legs and hands and face, and wonderful skin and hair, so you should be able to do well with those, and God knows, the camera adores you. Remember, in our school photos the rest of us invariably looked like gargoyles, but there you were, always exquisite. It used to make us all sick. As it happens, there's a big cosmetics firm that's going to make a push for the Pacific market, and they want a local model, somebody from here or Australia, but a woman with exotic looks who'll be suitable for the Asian market too.'

'I can't model.'

'Oh, of course you can. All you have to do is swan around looking glamorous, and you do that instinctively. You'd wing it, no problem, if they decided you were the one. They're being rather fussy, but you're interesting, and you're new, which they're rather keen on, and you'd certainly show off their stuff. You've got those wonderful eyes, and perfect cheekbones, and a mouth that might have been made to show off lipstick.'

'Jess, I know you mean well, but I've——'

'Don't say no yet. Look, it's not going to take much time. You'll be working like hell for six months or so all around the Pacific, but then it will be finished. You could send your CV around and apply for a proper job next year. It would get you out of New Zealand until the heat dies off, and it would certainly tip your bank balance the right way.'

It sounded seductive, but Aura couldn't make a decision yet. Vaguely she said, 'I'll see.'

'What you need,' Jessica said firmly, 'is time out.'

Aura smiled sardonically. 'Not a chance of it, I'm afraid.'

But that evening Laurel and Alick came along, offering her just that: as long as she liked at Kerikeri, or anywhere else for that matter.

Aura smiled. She had become very good at hiding her emotions behind a mask. 'You're so kind,' she said, 'but would you mind very much if I said no? Honestly, I'm not feeling madly social at the moment.'

Alick began to say something but Laurel broke in firmly. 'Of course we understand,' she said, 'but Natalie, you'll come up, won't you? It's been a while since we've had you there, and you really do need a change of scenery.'

Natalie sighed, and wept a little, and without looking at Aura agreed that a small holiday might be just what she needed, although of course she really adored the tropics at this time of year, and the fares to Fiji were so low right now...

When neither Laurel nor Alick reacted to this blatant attempt at manipulation she gave in with a good grace.

Aura felt as though a load had rolled from her mind. As Laurel and Alick left she gave them both a fierce hug and whispered her thanks.

'It's not too late to change your mind,' Alick said, returning the embrace. 'We'd love to have you, and the kids adore their cousin Aura.'

Aura shook her head. 'I adore them, too, but—not just now.'

Ten o'clock the next morning saw her waving them away in Alick's big car. On her way up the path her nose traced a faint, sweet smell. It was a tiny gold narcissus shaped just like a miniature hoop petticoat, blooming in the border she had weeded only a fortnight before. A fortnight before, when she had been going to become Paul's wife.

Perhaps it was a little omen, a promise that however bleak her days, hope was never lost.

Hope seemed to have become very much mislaid, however, in the days that followed. Aura missed Paul. She missed him alarmingly, missed his pleasant temperament, his humour, his never-failing thoughtfulness.

But she missed Flint with a hunger that ate deep into her bones, a desire almost physical in its intensity that coloured her days and darkened her nights with an ever-present ache of loneliness.

She didn't love him, not as she loved Paul, but some part of her was bereft.

Lust. An ugly word for an ugly emotion, if emotion it was. She wanted Flint, longed for the sensual pleasures he could give her, and despised herself for this obsession, because she didn't like him. She could respect his strength, admit his good qualities, appreciate his cold, hard intellect, but the man himself meant nothing to her.

On the day that was to have been her wedding she stayed at home. Jessica tried to persuade her to spend the weekend with her and Sam, but Aura refused, just as she refused Laurel's telephoned plea to go up to Kerikeri. Deliberately emptying her mind, she went about her chores racked with regret, with remorse and self-disgust.

During that weekend she made the decision to give Jessica's plan a try. Delighted, Jessica was immediately all business; she gave her the address of a photographer and introduced her to her partner, an alarmingly beautiful woman in her mid-thirties who Aura had met a couple of times before.

Apparently she approved. Eight days after she had handed in her portfolio Aura found herself ringing Alick for the name of his lawyer.

'What do you want a lawyer for?' he asked after he'd given it.

'Mind your own business,' she said automatically.

'I made you my business twenty years ago.'

She was already regretting her curtness. 'Sorry.'

When she had finished telling him he said, 'Hm. Are you sure you want to do it? I can lend you any money you need, you know.'

'I know, but it's time I stopped relying on you.'

'Well, don't let your pride stand in the way of common sense. By the way, Natalie's been prospecting up here, and unless I'm reading things wrong, she's getting her own future sorted out.'

'A man, I gather.' Aura hid the note of hope in her voice with dryness.

He laughed. 'Yes, a nice rich Canadian who thinks she's wonderful.'

Oh, if only it happened! Aura said guiltily, 'I hope he knows what he's doing.'

'I think he does. Don't worry about him, Aura, and don't worry about your mother, either. She'll fall on her feet.'

Life suddenly became at once simpler, and infinitely more complicated. The company and the agency took over her life. She met executives, got used to being looked at and discussed as though she were a piece of merchandise, attended a modelling course, and discovered that photographic sessions involved a lot of hard work and boredom.

At least she no longer had to worry about Natalie's debts. The money she received as an advance paid them off, and, following Alick's advice not to let pride stand in her way, she borrowed enough from him to keep herself going until the next payment was due.

Two months later she was in Cairns, posing against a swimming-pool in sunlight so bright she was glad it was just her legs they were photographing and not her face. This session was for sunscreens and moisturising lotions, and it was going well, as was the campaign.

It still surprised her that she, ordinary Aura Forsythe, photographed like a houri. Originally the job had been a means to an end, but now she was determined to give her employers value for the indecent amount of money they were paying her. At first she had worried about whether she could actually do the work, and been heartily relieved when word came back that they were delighted with the shots so far.

The actual work she still found dull, but fortunately the camera lens transformed her boredom into a profoundly seductive glower. She enjoyed the travel, and she liked the crew she was working with.

She should have been happy. Especially here, in Australia's tropical north, a place she'd always wanted to visit.

When the first day's work was finished she relaxed for a moment in the coolness of the hotel foyer. She had just tilted her head against the white cane back of the chair when she heard his voice.

'Thank you, that's all.'

Of course she was hallucinating, if you could do that with voices. It wasn't the first time this had happened; she had quite often 'seen' Flint, only to discover that the man bore no real resemblance beyond the most obvious aspects of height and build and colouring.

Fortunately for her sanity few men were as tall as Flint, or possessed his breadth of shoulder. Few had hair that exact shade of brown bordering on auburn; few moved with his lean ranginess and lethal power-packed grace, and even fewer had his unpressured, commanding air.

So she opened her eyes to prove herself wrong, and there he was, checking in at Reception. No other man had such a forceful profile, or a scar curling sinisterly down his tanned cheek. He towered over everyone else in the foyer, reducing them to nothingness, his hard-honed masculinity barely trammelled by the lightweight tropical suit he wore.

Aura's heart stopped. She didn't breathe, couldn't move; he had come, he had found her!

When he turned and casually scanned the foyer Aura almost sagged with pain, because clearly he hadn't known she was there. For a moment astonishment flared in the golden eyes, until he reimposed control and they turned to quartz, clear and depthless.

She was not going to fall apart, she was not going to make a fool of herself. It took all of her willpower, every tiny spark of it, to force herself to nod as he walked towards her, to stretch her lips in a smile.

'Aura,' he said with as little emotion in his tone as in his eyes.

The sound of her name on his lips gave her more pleasure than a hundred of the photographer's easy compliments. She inclined a serene, composed face towards him. A couple of months assuming expressions in front of the camera had given her much more confidence in her ability to hide her thoughts.

'Hello, Flint. What are you doing in Cairns?'

'Business,' he said briefly. He stood looking down at her with hooded eyes.

Several women passed in a laughing, chattering group, their glances flashing from one to the other, lingering on his impassive features. Aura had to fight the desire to send them on their way with a few scathing words.

'Has something gone wrong in Robertsons' operation here?' she asked lightly, wondering whether he could hear the intensity behind her words.

'Something did, but it's all right now.' He sat down opposite her. 'What are you doing?'

She shrugged, and told him.

'Modelling?' He didn't try to hide his surprise. 'You have the face for it, but I thought you had to be six feet tall and built like a greyhound.'

'I'm modelling for a range of cosmetics. All they need is a face and legs and skin,' she told him casually.

His brows lifted. 'Are you enjoying it?'

'It's a living.'

'I imagine you'd be very good at it,' he said, and it wasn't a compliment.

Her answering smile was ironic. 'Thank you,' she said sweetly.

Nothing had changed. He still thought she was nothing but a money-grubbing little opportunist, out for what she could get. No doubt he considerd modelling to be another way of selling herself.

'How long are you here for?'

She said, 'Another day. You?'

'I'm leaving tomorrow morning.' He smiled, and his eyes glinted as they slowly searched her face. 'Have dinner with me tonight,' he said.

Of course she should refuse, and of course she didn't. She might not love him, not as she loved Paul, but instead of being weakened by absence the strange, physical enchantment that imprisoned them both in its unseen snare had strengthened into an unholy sorcery. She could taste her need on her tongue, feel it throb through every cell in her body.

'I'll meet you in the bar at seven,' he said, getting to his feet in one smooth motion.

Although convinced that she might just have made the greatest mistake in her life, Aura nodded.

Back in her room she looked at herself, and sighed. Her eyes were brilliant and huge in her face, the pupils dilated into wildness. Even her lips seemed to have altered, grown soft and hungrily sultry.

She had learned ways of putting on cosmetics that dramatised her physical assets, and after she showered she used them, outlining her eyes with subtle precision, colouring her mouth carefully. Her hair she swept up to give her a bit more height; she picked a frangipani flower from the floating bowl in her bathroom and tucked it into the swirl on top of her head, pleased that the satiny petals with their golden throat contrasted effectively with its burgundy lights.

She chose a plain dress the exact colour of her eyes, letting its soft draping do all the emphasising necessary.

When she was ready she surveyed her reflection in the mirror. She looked a different woman from the one who had been engaged to Paul; she looked—glamorous, she thought with a faint smile. Almost decadent.

The hotel was small, elegantly making the most of its location on a tropical lagoon, much of the public area open to the warm, fragrant air. Before she reached the lifts she stopped and looked out across the fairy lights in the exquisite, palm-haunted garden. Unknown, sensual perfumes floated on the sultry air. Excitement bubbled within her, keen and poignant.

She was not naïve enough to believe in any future for them. He didn't love her, just as she didn't love him. But they were both free agents.

He was waiting for her in the bar, but so, unfortunately, were the rest of the photographic crew. They waved; Aura smiled and waved back, but headed steadily towards Flint.

Getting to his feet, he gave her a narrowed, unsmiling look. 'Do you want to join your friends?' he asked.

'If you want to meet them it's all right by me.'

'Not particularly.' His voice was indifferent to the point of rudeness. He waited until she had sat down before saying, 'What would you like to drink?'

'Dry white wine, please.'

'You won't get New Zealand whites here, but if you'll trust me I should be able to find you one you'll like.'

'Yes, of course I trust you.'

It sounded oddly like a vow, a promise. He gave the order to the waiter who had appeared the instant Flint looked up—he had that effect on waiters—then sat back and looked her over.

'You look different,' he said, the rasp in his voice more blatant. 'It's amazing, but you're even more beautiful than you were when I saw you last.'

The beginnings of a blush stained Aura's cheeks. 'Tricks of the trade,' she said dismissively. 'It's amazing what you can do with cosmetics.'

'Then I suppose I should be flattered that you took the time to use them, but I can remember seeing you with no make-up on at all, and you were just as stunningly beautiful.'

The blush heated into a fullblown wave of colour. He laughed quietly, and as the drinks arrived changed the subject, slipping with polished ease into an approximation of the pleasant chit-chat of old friends. Picking up her glass, Aura noted that he had ordered the same wine for himself, and sipped the delicately flavoured liquid with interest.

'How long have you been here?' she asked. He had been right about the wine—it was delicious; but then wine was clearly his hobby as well as his future.

'I got here at the crack of dawn this morning.'

Aura lifted her lashes. 'You keep long hours.' Not a hint of desolation, of anger because he hadn't contacted her, of the pain his defection had caused, disturbed the calmness of her voice.

Something of the forceful assurance of the man showed through for a moment. 'It's part of the job. In this case somebody panicked over nothing so I had very little to do. How long have you been here?'

'A day.'

'Where do you go when you've finished with Cairns? Back to Auckland?'

'Bali,' she said. 'I believe I have to pose draped over a water buffalo, and then wade through a rice paddy or two.'

'Be careful of water buffaloes, they don't like Westerners' smell.' He gave a white, ironic smile. 'There are some truly impressive rice paddies there. Whole hills, mountains almost, terraced by heaven knows how many people over the centuries.'

Aura, who had travelled very little, envied him his experience, although, she thought fleetingly, she didn't envy the cynicism that hardened his eyes, or the lines it had bracketed on either side of his mouth. Not that they detracted from his appeal; in a strange way they added to it.

He didn't talk about his job at all, but they drifted from scenery into politics, and she realised that he had a grasp of the inner workings of many other countries that could only come from an insider's understanding.

They had never sat like this, just talking, ignoring the blazing pull of the senses. She enjoyed it very much. Paul rarely discussed politics with her; he said that he spent all day thinking, he wanted to relax his brain when he came home. Aura had thought this entirely natural. Until that moment she hadn't realised how much she had missed the ebb and flow of conversation, the exhilaration of sharpening her wits against others equally keen.

When at last the wine was finished, he said, 'I thought you might like to go to a restaurant a few miles away in the rainforest. The food is superb, and the place itself is interesting.'

'It sounds lovely.'

They went by taxi, drawing up outside a two storeyed building, the upper floor supported by massive wooden columns. Beside the steps great pots stood, some with plants burgeoning in them, most empty, their superb shapes and glazes harmonising with the building and the setting. Creepers festooned down, flaunting brilliant flowers in a variety of forms and hues. Plants with monstrous foliage, huge leaves cut and slashed into a myriad shapes, added to the tropical ambience, the air of otherwordliness. Around them the trees of the rainforest pressed closely.

'It's like a jungle hideaway,' Aura exclaimed in delight.

'I think that's the impression the owners wanted to achieve.'

Until that moment Flint hadn't touched her, but he took her elbow as they climbed the steps, and the touch of those lean fingers sent a feverish tremor up her arm and straight to her heart.

She sent him a swift sideways look. What would it be like to live with him, to share the mundane things of life, a bathroom, breakfast, weeding the garden, washing the dishes? Heaven, she thought hollowly. It would be heaven.

The restaurant was small, the tables rough-hewn wood; the chairs, however, were extremely comfortable, and the food, a marvellous combination of South-East Asian flavours with European, wonderful.

Over dinner they talked of everything, of books, of films, their likings in art. Yet although she was singingly happy, almost exalted, Aura hungered for more personal subjects; she wanted to know so much about him, things he had no intention of revealing.

Crushing the useless, wishful need, she set out to enjoy this evening, because this was all she would ever have of him: dinner in this restaurant, his conversation, and the hidden yet compelling tug of attraction that seemed to be binding her ever tighter, ever more helplessly, in its coils.

'How *did* you get that scar?' she asked over coffee, spinning out the time.

He gave her a sardonic look. 'When I was fifteen I was carrying a coil of number eight fencing wire across a paddock. A hen pheasant flew up from under my feet. I tripped, and the wire-end caught my cheek.'

Aura grinned, her eyes glinting mischievously. He laughed, wryly amused.

'It looks very piratical,' she said. Perhaps it was the wine, or perhaps just the magic of the evening, but now she was bold enough to follow with her forefinger the thin line from his cheekbone to the sharper angle of his jaw. As her finger quested down it tingled at the slight abrasion of his beard and the heat of his skin.

Eyes gleaming, he waited until she had reached the end, then pressed his hand over hers and kissed her palm, his tongue tracing the slight indentation of her life line.

Silently he asked a question. Colour heated her cheeks. Silently she answered it. He put her hand down and looked across the room, summoning the waiter.

Without speaking she sat beside him as the taxi drove through the sweet darkness to the hotel. She waited while he paid the taxi off, went with him into the foyer of the hotel and across to the lifts. There were a couple of other people in their car, so they didn't speak until they were in the corridor.

'I have a suite. I think we'll be more comfortable there,' he said.

Aura froze. For a moment her brain balked, scraps of thoughts floating through it.

Oh, I want to—he'll think me a slut—he already thinks I wanted to marry Paul for his money...

'Yes, all right,' she said composedly.

Nothing, she thought with a bleak humour that surprised her, could be as wonderful as she imagined making love with Flint to be, so it was bound to disappoint her. And then, perhaps, she'd be able to get on with her life and find a man she both loved and wanted.

His face impassive, Flint unlocked his door, then stood back to let her go through.

Already Aura was regretting her decision, but the reasons for making it still held. She was tired of being bound on the rack of her own desires. She wanted to sate them, and by exhausting them be free once more.

His room was bigger than hers. Neater, too. Apart from a briefcase set beside the desk there was no sign of his presence. A half open door on the far wall revealed a huge bed.

'Would you like something to drink?' he asked.

She shook her head. The frangipani blossom in her hair fell to the floor, and she stooped to pick it up, holding the warm thing in the palm of her hand. 'I don't really want a drink,' she said under her breath.

'What do you want?' His voice was just as quiet.

Aura's fingers contracted and the flower was crushed, although its fragrance lingered on her skin. Turning, she dropped it into a wastepaper basket.

'Must I spell it out?' she asked in a low voice.

'No.' He came up behind her, and took her shoulders in his hands, drawing her back against his chest. The curtains weren't drawn so she could see their reflections in the glass, she small and pale in contrast to the wide shoulders of the man who held her, his darkly intent face turned, as was hers, to the window.

The slow movement of his thumbs over the slender bones of her shoulder, the soft warmth of his breath stirring the tendrils of hair, the heat and promise of strength that emanated from the lean graceful body behind her—all joined to set strange tides pulsing through her.

'Why?' he asked levelly.

Her shoulders lifted in the smallest of shrugs. 'Why did you ask me? Does it matter?'

'No, I suppose not. We both knew we had unfinished business together.' He turned her and looked down into her face with unveiled appreciation, his eyes pure flame.

Aura felt that look burn through her, so that the old Aura, the woman who hadn't understood that passion could be a living force, sloughed away like a paper skin, curling and twisting into the uniquiet past. She had never before felt so much part of a moment, so vividly, hectically aware of this moment, this man, this room.

'You are so beautiful,' he said levelly. 'You tear my heart out, do you know that? I look at you, and I'm unmanned, a supplicant at the gate of your beauty. Are you going to let me in, Aura?'

His words affected her so powerfully that she couldn't speak. There was nothing personal in his desire, merely a detached male hunger for beauty, the need to make it his, to assume command over it and by doing so lessen its impact.

But that was what she wanted, too. That was why she was there. His simple, stark statement of passion shook her as florid protestations could never do. Appalled and excited in equal parts by his honesty, she nodded. By satisfying his desire and hers she could at least give him something, although it wouldn't be the one thing she wanted to give him. He wouldn't take her love.

For of course this passionate attraction she had so despised was not just lust. It was love. She loved this man as she had never loved Paul. Paul had been the answer the lonely, forsaken child in her had sought, the man who would be loyal and never leave her, never let her be lonely and unsure again.

What she felt for Flint so far surpassed that need to be protected that the two desires had nothing in common.

'Yes,' she said, and reached up her arms and brought his face down to meet hers, his mouth to touch hers.

For a moment he stood still, long enough for her to wonder whether he was so dominant that he needed to take the lead at all times. Then his arms tightened around her and she knew that she had been wrong. He kissed her with elemental, white-hot hunger, immediately taking advantage of her silent gasp to thrust deep and sensually into the sweet depths he found.

Her knees gave way, and still with his mouth on hers he picked her up and carried her through to the bed, tearing his mouth free only to bury his face in her throat for a moment. His eyes caught and held hers as he slid her down his body, revealing as nothing else could his state of arousal.

Aura gasped again, and his hard mouth tilted crookedly. 'You drive me insane,' he said roughly. 'No other woman has ever been able to make me hard just by looking at me. Do I do that to you, Aura, with your hair like a burgundy flame and your green, green eyes set like jewels in your black lashes?' His fingers found the hidden zip of her dress and worked it down. 'Does your body tighten, and your breath hurt your lungs, and your heart beat like a kettledrum in your ears?'

The dress came loose; he flipped it over her head and looked at the rich treasure revealed to him, smooth ivory curves of breast and waist and hips, the plane of her stomach with its seductive dimple, the narrow silk briefs that hindered further exploration.

Those intense, half-closed eyes surveyed her with intimate thoroughness, lingering on the rosy-apricot aureoles of her breasts until they hardened into tiny nubs, tiptilted, provocative. Wildfire zigzagged through her, uniting between the fork of her legs into a conflagration. She had never felt so exposed, so vulnerable, and she had never realised that she could enjoy such an experience.

'Undress me,' he said harshly.

No doubt it would have been more suitable to a virgin if her fingers had trembled and been unable to undo the little buttons of his shirt, but they didn't. Swiftly, competently, they moved down crisp white material that was warm from his body heat, then pushed the sleeves back over his shoulders, pulling them down until the shirt dropped on to the floor.

Dry-mouthed, she stared at him. For the first time a hint of panic darkened her eyes. He was overwhelming, the male predator incarnate, with his wide bronze shoulders and chest where the hair curled in evocative patterns over smooth muscles, hinting at the disturbing, elemental power concealed there. Yet there was something intensely tantalising about him too. Aura touched the bold parabola of a muscle with her finger, then spread her hand to catch the heavy thud of his heart in her palm.

His skin was like oiled silk, warm and slightly clinging to her sensitive fingertips, smooth and sleek and potent. Aura leaned forward and applied the tip of her tongue to the spot she had touched. Beneath her hand she felt his pulse speed up; his chest lifted as he dragged air into his lungs. An oblique smile tilted her lips. Like a small cat she licked along the line of a muscle, tasting the musky, salty tang of aroused male, of Flint.

She half expected him to say something, to stop her, but he didn't move, held still by an effort she barely recognised.

'You taste—of heaven,' she said.

He laughed deep in his throat and said, 'And what do you taste of, I wonder?'

He lifted her, and stripped off the sleek silk briefs, then pushed his own clothes free. Aura's eyes dilated. She swallowed and stopped an involuntary gasp by sheer force of will. He was so big, and so——

She knew it was possible, but she didn't see how it could happen.

He must have realised the source of her sudden dismayed silence, for as he came down beside her he said quietly, 'We'll take it easy,' and before she could answer he lowered his head and kissed the tender upper curve of her breast. His mouth lingered, as though the taste of her skin excited him as much as his did her.

'Yes, you taste like the essence of woman,' he said against her skin. 'Sweeter than violets and more potent than brandy. You make me drunk.'

Aura's breath came hard and fast through lips already reddened by his kisses. More than anything she wanted to experience again the ecstasy of the moments in his apartment when he had touched her, and kissed her, and her whole being had risen to meet his.

CHAPTER SEVEN

BUT he was in no hurry. He held back, reimposing a fierce control over his emotions and actions, his hands moving slowly and tormentingly across her skin.

Outside a bird called from the lagoon, unknown, alien. Aura shivered as much with a sense of doom, of no going back, as with the wild pleasure that was coursing through her.

'You have a mouth made to kiss, made to crush, made for me,' he said softly, holding the weight of one breast in the palm of his hand. He looked at it with the awe and possessiveness of a man who holds infinite value in his grasp. 'And skin like ivory satin.'

Transfixed by the smouldering light in his eyes, she held her breath. He spoke a lover's words, yet they were not delivered in a lover's voice, and the look in his eyes was not tender.

Unease widened her eyes; then she gasped as he kissed a hard, tight little nipple, and taking it into the warm cavity of his mouth suckled strongly.

Sensation, swift and heated as fire, smooth and sweet as honey, shot through her. She closed her eyes, unable to cope with the feelings he aroused, unable to watch his mouth work its primal magic, unable to bear the contrast between the blunt angles of his dark face and the smooth pale curves of her body.

Utterly ravished by need, she sighed his name.

'Touch me,' he said against the curve of her breast, taking her hand and holding it over his heart.

She explored him as he explored her, amazed afresh at the polished swell of muscles that flexed in response to her tentative hands. Each touch, each caress, each new step on the voyage of discovery added to the last, extended the next, until in the end his fingers slid carefully down and discovered her secret core, eager and hot, awaiting him.

Aura's lashes flew up. His heavy-lidded gaze was fixed on her face in a scrutiny that held all the old watchfulness. If she winced, or tensed, he would wonder why, and perhaps guess.

And that would be the finish. He didn't want a virgin in his bed, he wanted a woman with experience, a woman who could match his expertise. She couldn't give him that, but she would give him something she could only surrender once.

She turned her head into his chest, and delicately bit at the tight nubbin she found there. A deep breath expanded his chest, then his hand slipped a little further, sending shivers of delight through her. His thumb moved, found the centre of pleasure, and she shuddered.

'Yes, you want me,' he said softly. 'How much do you want me, Aura?'

She lifted weighted lashes and said on a sigh, 'More than anything.'

'More than anything?' He laughed and turned away.

For a horrified moment she assumed he was rejecting her as he had before. Even as she formulated the thought she realised what he was doing. There would be no unwanted child from this mating.

Seconds later, one sure movement brought him over her completely, the powerful body, beautiful in its uncompromising masculinity poised, gathering strength, until he said harshly, '*Now*,' and took her in a single powerful thrust that pressed smoothly home.

Later she would think that the first moment of possession changed her fundamentally; at the time, she was so anxious in case he found some evidence of her virginity that she didn't really appreciate what had happened. But after that moment of union he stopped, almost as though he waited for her to do something.

As Aura's wondering eyes, dilated and languorous, almost afraid, took in his clenched jaw and stark bone-structure, she realised two things: he was fighting for control, and in the silken sheath that surrounded him there was no betraying impediment. She was able to relax, and the responses her anxiety had blocked out roared back into her consciousness,.

A feeling of fullness, of completeness, was strengthened by a return of the overpowering excitement he had coaxed from her with his expert manipulation of her body. She stretched languidly, acutely conscious of his immediate, quickly leashed reaction. A desire to show him that he couldn't control everything led her to move her hips experimentally.

'No,' he said harshly.

'Why?' Her voice was quiet in the quiet room, slow and deep and husky. 'Don't you like it?'

He gave an odd groan. 'I like it too much. No, damn you, don't! If you want me to be any good for you, just lie still.'

She tried, but as he moved, establishing a leisurely rhythm of advance and withdrawal as the scent of their lovemaking and the tactile delight of skin against skin, as his skill and strength fanned the flames of passion, a disturbance rioted through her, carrying her into an unknown region where all that mattered was reaching some unattainable objective.

Racked by a feverish need to know, a consuming hunger, taken over by something greater than anything she had ever experienced before, Aura was heedless of everything but the mindless, sugar-sweet tide of delight that raced through her and the beloved weight pressing her loins into the bed, the slow penetration of her innermost secrets.

Until that moment she had never thought of herself as passionate; she had believed her sultry face and slender body were at bewildering variance with her nature. But now, locked in the most primal embrace of all, giving with all her heart and body, taking just as eagerly, she was forced to accept that these frenzied moments when the dark fire built higher and higher, when every sense was sharpened to an acuity almost painful, were what she had been born for.

She looked up at the man above her and inside her, crying out with pleasure because she was not the only one in thrall to this consuming, primal heat.

Flint's skin was drawn tight over the fierce bone structure of his face, beads of sweat stood out across his brow; his mouth was hard, almost snarling as he muttered, 'Aura, I can't—dear God——'

The slow, almost teasing movements of his body were suddenly transmuted into fierce thrusts. His head jerked back, and as she watched, her pleasure immeasurably heightened by his, tension snapped inside her, flinging her through waves of ecstasy into a rapturous present that had no beginning and no end, into a place where she was stripped to her barest essentials, where this violent and elemental sensation was all that mattered.

He groaned her name, and his body tightened and she was pierced by wonder and awe when the ripples of her own climax swept back up into waves to meet his and match it.

She heard her voice, shook to the beat of her heart, and thought she might die of pleasure. And then he collapsed, the tension in the long muscles slackened, the proud body at last brought low by satiation.

Aura lay in his arms, holding him in her turn like a precious burden. Very slowly, so slowly that there was never a moment when she first realised it, she discovered that it didn't really matter that this man who lay breathing deeply in her arms, his heart thundering against hers, who had possessed her in a way transcending the physical...that this man was more dangerous to her than the tiger she saw in him could ever be. She could never trust his loyalty, nor that he would always be around for her. But she loved him.

She had fought a valiant action against that love, clinging to her childhood need for stability, longing to be protected and cared for, longing for a father. It was strange how the wildness inside her had known better than she did what she needed. Something in Flint's lawless character had chimed with hers.

A small, replete smile touched a mouth softly swollen by his kisses. Aura was overwhelmed by an ecstasy that had little to do with the physical satisfaction enfolding her body in such lethargic pleasure. So this, she thought wonderingly, was what it felt like to love, to be helpless before its power.

It was as far removed from the affection she had felt for Paul as an eagle was from a sparrow. It was magnificent, and yet it was mundane too; she wanted to live with Flint, to see him in the morning when he was unshaven and the sexy roughness of his voice was transformed by the night's disuse to a rasp, to laugh with him over something small and insignificant, but important because it was part of their shared life. She wanted to argue with him and love him and look after him, and be looked after in her turn.

It didn't even seem to matter that he felt nothing like this for her.

She turned her head, her heart melting at his closed eyes, the relaxed contours of his face. She had done this for him.

The long lashes quivered, and slowly lifted to reveal golden eyes as cool and enigmatic as the transparent heart of a crystal.

'I must weigh a ton,' he said, and eased himself over on to his back.

She wanted to cry out, but a strong arm swept her close and held her with her arm across his lean waist, her cheek on his chest.

The lights glimmered against the perfumed darkness outside. Wrapped in a contentment so profound it seemed like Nirvana, Aura lay against the man she had learned too late she would give her life for, and let her mind drift.

Before long she was asleep.

She woke some time before dawn, but it wasn't the lightening sky that woke her, or the songs of birds she had never heard before. It was the gentle touch of Flint's hand on her breast, and the sound of his quickening breath in the quiet room.

She said drowsily, 'Flint?'

'Who did you think it might be? No, don't tell me.' His voice was husky, and his caress became a statement of possession. Almost before she had time to react he bent his head and kissed her answer from her mouth. 'You look so rare and precious and exquisite in my bed,' he said against her lips.

Fighting the instant leap in her blood, Aura levered her eyelids upwards. He was an outline in the dim room, the sloping line of his shoulders blocking out most of the faint light that filtered through the pavilion of mosquito net shutting them off from the world. Again she was awed by his size, and then heartened by memories, for last night they had fitted perfectly, her smallness taking him and enveloping him as if it had been meant.

It was going to happen again; she could sense his determination with her skin, with the infinitesimal receptors that had once been of use in the days when humans had no language.

'Aura?' he murmured.

She drew a shallow breath and said, 'Yes.'

It was answer enough.

There was no repeat of the passionate, almost frenzied haste of the night before. This time he touched her confidently, and the slow progress of his hands over her skin sent imperative messages to the melting centre of her passion. It was different because she knew what he could do to her, she knew what was to come, and instead of dulling her expectation the knowledge increased it.

This time, made bold by recollection, she was more forward, discovering with lazy, sleepy excitement that his skin pulled taut beneath her questing strokes, that when she bit gently at his shoulders he shivered.

Natalie believed that men were far more interested in sex than women; she said it was one of the things women had to put up with in exchange for security and companionship. A child of her time, Aura had read magazines and books and knew with the logical part of her mind that this was not so, that making love should be equally pleasurable for both sexes.

But it had taken Flint's passionate overwhelming of her defences last night to convince her emotionally. Now that she knew it was true, she prepared to abandon herself to her senses, to explore and enjoy his body as he so clearly did hers. Investigating him with a cold candour, she ranged over his sleek hide with a murmurous delight in all the things that were different.

She sensed that he wasn't accustomed to being touched quite so familiarly, and her fingers stilled.

But he said, 'No, don't stop.'

'You are so beautiful,' she said, turning her face into his flat stomach.

It expanded as he laughed. 'That's the first time anyone's used that term for me.'

She tasted the skin there, nibbling along a rib until he pushed her mouth away and pulled her up to kiss it.

'Now you,' he said quietly against her lips, '*you're* beautiful, but you know that, don't you. Other men have told you often enough. Have they told you that when you smile your eyes gleam, and you have a maddening way of lowering your lashes?'

'No,' she said, as his mouth roved the smooth length of her throat.

'Nobody? What a hopeless set. You were made for love, Aura. Your breasts fit into a man's hands as though they had been made for him, and whenever I look at those amazing legs I imagine them wrapped around me, holding me tightly, and my whole body clenches. But the reality is so much more spectacular than all my imaginings.'

For the first time since she was fourteen she didn't shrink with a cold nausea at the thought of being part of a man's fantasies. The sound of Flint's gravelly voice sent her pulses careering, banished forever the taint that one man's perversion had imprinted on her memory.

'Your palms have an innocent, unprotected look,' he murmured, 'just like the insides of your elbows. As for that tormenting place where your neck meets your shoulders, and the little hollow in your throat, and...'

He kissed each place he mentioned, stroked across heated skin with slow fingers, tantalising her with the contrast between his rough voice and his gentle touch, his blazing sexuality and the intense restraint that fettered it.

Desire burned with metallic lustre in his eyes, captured his mouth and forced it into a straight line. Although he continued to drug her with dark words of passion his lips hardly moved, yet his hands shook.

And when she kissed him, when she touched him in her turn, she could see the involuntary secret imprint of her fingers, her mouth, on his skin, in the building heat that scorched through them both.

When at last he groaned, 'I want you—Aura, I want you *now*,' she was eagerly compliant—no, there was nothing of compliance in the way she moved, inciting him, tormenting in her turn, moving over him so that he lay beneath her like a sacrificial victim, bronzed skin gleaming with a faint dew of sweat that would mingle with hers.

'Now?' she said, and before he had time to answer, she slid over him, taking him into her.

It didn't hurt, but for a second she froze, her eyes dilated, her body thrumming like a guitar-string with sensations so acute she thought she might faint.

'Aura——'

She couldn't stay still. The fire in her blood hurtled her along a path of unhindered eroticism; she lowered her face to kiss his hard mouth, burgundy hair falling like a warm curtain of silk around his face, and with a skill that was new and untried gave herself up to an innocent, sweet carnality.

When it was over she thought dazedly that she had never expected it to be like that. People tried to describe it, but there were no words, no ways...

She yawned, and he laughed. 'Got to sleep,' he said deeply.

Aura didn't think she could ever sleep again, but she did, while outside the dawn sky lightened into the warmth of a tropical winter, and the man beneath her lay with his arms around her slender form and his eyes wide open, staring at the ceiling.

The dream started innocuously. She was laughing up at Paul, her ring winking on her finger, while they were dancing to a Strauss waltz. 'The Blue Danube'.

'It isn't blue, of course,' Paul told her, smiling. 'The Danube is really a muddy brown,' and then he tripped, and she realised that there was a hole in the floor, a hole that got bigger, with Paul teetering on the edge of it, a hole that ate through the floorboards and became a black pit where things gibbered and waited.

Paul's face was distorted with terror; he called her name, and she clung, trying to hold him back from the pit. In the background the band continued to play, and everyone else danced sedately around the edges, ignoring the pit and the dreadful things waiting there and Paul's struggles, even though he was trembling on the brink.

Aura couldn't scream; whimpering, she tried to drag him free, but he slid through her fingers and inexorably into the darkness, and she called desperately, 'Paul, don't go—Paul, hang on—Paul Paul Paul Paul...'

But someone was shaking her, someone was hauling her away, and as she struggled, Paul disappeared into the darkness, his eyes fixed despairingly on her, and she burst into harsh sobs that tore her to pieces.

'Wake up! Aura, stop it, you're having a nightmare!'

She opened desperate eyes. After a horrified moment they focused on Flint's face. She heard Paul's name dying on her lips, echoing in the quiet room.

'It's all right,' Flint said, and tried to pull her into his arms, but she huddled away against the pillow, holding herself rigid.

Something bleak moved in the depths of his eyes, but he said evenly, 'It was just a dream, Aura. A nightmare. I'll get you a drink.'

Shuddering, she tried to dispel the lingering miasma of the nightmare. By the time he came back from the bathroom with a glass of water she had almost succeeded. With one hand she pushed tangled hair back from her face, with the other she clutched the glass. Her teeth chattered, but she managed to drink the water down without spilling it.

He took the glass from her, flicked away the cloud of netting and sat down on the side of the bed. Now, when it was too late, she wanted him to hold her, to convince her that she had nothing to fear, but she couldn't make the first move. He was distant, wrapped in a remoteness she couldn't penetrate.

'All right now?' he asked her.

Not trusting her voice, she nodded.

'Do you get them often?'

'No.' It came out creaky, but at least it was usable. She hesitated, then said, 'It's the first time it's ever happened to me.'

'And no prizes for telling what caused it.'

She bit her lip, because of course she knew what had brought it on. Her unconscious mind was accusing her of the betrayal she had committed. Making love with Paul's best friend had been the final straw.

'I'm all right,' she said, staring down at the sheet, keeping her gaze there by sheer force of will because she couldn't bear to look at his calm, reasonable expression.

'I didn't realise you were so badly affected by—the break-up.' His voice was steady, uninflected.

She shook her head. 'It doesn't matter now. It's over.'

'It's clearly not over for you,' he said, still in that same impersonal tone.

She sat mutely as he got to his feet and went across to the window. A swift, angry movement of one strong brown hand looped back the thin curtains. That hand, and her memories of what it had done to her during the night, made Aura flush, warmed her a little against the misery of the dream. But their lovemaking now seemed just as unreal as the images her mind had called up from the pit of her secret fears.

It meant nothing to Flint but the appeasing of an appetite; he had told her that she was beautiful, told her what her beauty did to him, but he hadn't spoken a word that could be construed to be loving.

Aura looked away. Outside the world was flooded with heat and light, but there was grey desolation in her heart, a disillusion as heavy and foreboding as the bleakest thundercloud.

'I'd better get back to my room,' she said drearily, struggling to her feet and looking about for her clothes.

He said, 'What are you going to do?' There was nothing but an impersonal concern in his voice.

Aura couldn't wait to get away. As she climbed into her clothes she said, very fast, 'Go on to Bali, and then back home.'

'Will you be seeing Paul?'

Her fingers stilled on the catch of her bra. She looked over to where he stood looking out the window. The bluntly arrogant outline of his profile was etched against the soft blue wall; the sun summoned copper lights from his hair. He was a glowing statue in the tropical light, with all a statue's warmth.

'No,' she said, shivering.

'It's probably just as well.'

Desperate to get away, she pulled her dress over her head and stuffed her stockings into her handbag, sliding arched bare feet into high-heeled sandals.

'Goodbye,' she said bleakly, heading for the door.

He looked at her then. For a hopeful moment Aura searched his unyielding features, then turned away, welcoming the numb acceptance that replaced the aching loneliness. In his face, in his eyes, there was nothing but guarded detachment, as though he expected her to make a fuss.

Pride stiffened her back, brought a smile to her pale lips.

'Aura——'

The smile solidified, but was maintained. 'It was good. Let's leave it like that,' she said, opening the door and closing it behind her with a sharp, final click.

Fortunately there was no one else in the corridor. Back in her room she showered, but even as the water washed away his scent from her body, and toothpaste banished his taste from her mouth, she knew that what had happened the night before had been irrevocable. For him it might only be a one-night stand, but for her it had been commitment. In the most basic way of all, she felt that he belonged to her just as she now belonged to him.

The white towel clung not unpleasantly to her body. At least, she thought wearily, I don't have to worry much about being pregnant.

He had taken care of that both times.

Bali was hot, and the water buffalo didn't want anything to do with her, only reluctantly yielding to its master's determinaton. The emerald paddy fields were truly monuments to the skill of generations of men.

At any other time Aura would have enjoyed it. As it was, she went through the motions wrapped in a grey fog of despair that fortunately translated on film to a look of exotic sensuality.

When she got back to Auckland it was still raining, and there had clearly been no one in the unit for some time. Sighing, because Natalie had been in Kerikeri too often these last months, she rang Alick's phone number.

Laurel answered, her cool voice warming when she heard Aura's greeting. 'How was Cairns?' she asked.

'It didn't rain once while I was there.'

'And Bali?'

'One or two showers. Nothing like this.'

Alick's wife laughed. 'Come on, it doesn't rain all the time here.'

'No, it just seems like it. Is Natalie still with you?'

Laurel's voice altered subtly, although it was still warm. 'Yes. She has some news for you. I'll get her.'

Natalie's voice was velvet with satisfaction. 'Darling, I'm getting married,' she said brightly.

'Oh.' The Canadian?

'He's a darling, you'll love him. He's over here organising a farm he's bought halfway between Whangarei and the coast.'

'Natalie, are you sure?'

'Yes, I am sure. Very sure. We're having a quiet little wedding up here in Kerikeri—Lauren's dealing with everything, bless her——' and Alick's paying for it, Aura thought cynically '—and then we're going on a trip around the world. You'll be able to come and see us, darling. Joe lives quite close to Calgary.'

Aura was willing to bet that her mother had never heard of Calgary until she met Joe, but she spoke of it now as though it was the hub of the universe.

Hoping fervently that both Natalie and Joe knew what they were doing, she went up to Kerikeri two days before the wedding, and soon realised that Joe Donaldson knew exactly what he was in for. She also discovered, to her astonishment, that Natalie was in love.

'Amazing, isn't it?' her mother confided, looking younger and even more extravagantly beautiful. 'I thought that after your father——'

'Did you love him?' Aura had often wondered.

'Oh, yes.' Natalie smoothed down a lock of hair, gazing at her reflection with eyes that saw into the past. 'And we were happy, until he decided that Africa was more important than his family. I knew that I'd never cope with Africa, but he insisted we go with him. Sometimes there are situations where no amount of compromising will work. He had a vocation. I didn't go with him, but I loved him, and he loved me.'

'So why on earth did you marry Lionel Helswell?'

Natalie shrugged. 'He—oh, he promised to look after me, and although I know it's not what women of your generation are supposed to want, that's what I was brought up to expect in a marriage. That's the way I am. It's too late for me to change now, Aura.'

'Yes, I suppose it is.' Aura smiled.

'Joe's not like Lionel, Aura.'

No, the thin, shrewd, cheerful cattle rancher and oilman was nothing like her other stepfather. His good heart was patently revealed whenever he spoke. Aura thought that this time her mother had chosen well. 'I hope you'll be happy,' she said.

'I will be. What about you?'

Aura smiled steadily. 'I'm fine.'

Natalie was Natalie. Because she was happy, she assumed everyone else would be. 'Well, all's well that ends well. Promise me you'll keep in touch.'

'Of course I will.'

'You'll be able to come and see us whenever you like. And you have Laurel and Alick if things go wrong. Laurel is very fond of you.'

Aura smiled painfully. 'I'm a big girl now.'

Her mother laughed, and sprayed the air with perfume, walking through it so that it clung to her in a faint, subtle mist of fragrance. 'Oh, life is wonderful,' she said happily.

Back in Auckland Aura organised the sale of the unit, then moved into a big old Kauri villa in Mt Eden with five other women, and for the first time since boarding school found herself coping with communal living. She enjoyed the company and the casual camaraderie, and the conversation and activity kept her from feeling too lonely.

The advertising campaign hit the magazines and newspapers and to her surprise she became a minor celebrity, interviewed by journalists and offered work she didn't want, and couldn't take anyway because her contract was exclusive.

'It's those eyes,' Jessica told her cheerfully as she riffled through pages of proofs. 'They photograph wonderfully, all sultry allure and mischief. The coloured contact lenses were a brilliant idea. I don't know how you manage to look innocent in brown and earnest in blue, but it works.'

'The camera lies,' Aura said shortly. She wandered across Jessica's office and stared out of the window. Sunlight danced on the Waitemata Harbour, lovingly delineated the curves of island and peninsula and bay, picked out the corrugated iron roofs of the houses on the North Shore. A frigate was in dock at the naval base, and the two little green volcanoes in Devonport rose like exotic Christmas puddings above the sleek grey ship.

'It doesn't lie, it just loves your face, and your hands, and your legs. Actually, it loves you. If you were four inches taller and half a stone lighter you'd make a fortune.'

'I don't want a fortune. And I don't want any work when this runs out. I want to work at the job I've been trained for.' Aura knew she sounded abrupt, but she was becoming desperate. An aching grief was eating away at her heart.

More than anything she wanted to be able to get her teeth into some hard work, the sort of mental exercise that would force her to snap out of this slough of self-pity she seemed permanently immured in. She had bought another computer and spent as much time as she could working at it, but the interest and excitement seemed to have faded into the same dull greyness that tainted all of her life now.

'I think you're mad,' Jessica said comfortably. 'Although I'm not surprised. You were always as stubborn as a pig. How are things going?'

Aura knew what she meant. 'I'm surviving,' she said lightly.

'I saw Paul at a book launch the other night.'

'How did he look?'

'Grim. About as grim as you do when you think no one's looking.'

Aura's brows knotted together.

'Don't frown,' Jessica said automatically. 'It helps to talk, you know.'

'I've already bored you once.'

'Don't be an idiot. Just remember, I'm always here. Oh, there's an article about Flint Jansen in the latest *Wine and Food*. It seems he's going to stick his neck out and make wine on the coast out from Warkworth.

houses had been built, far enough away not to be obtrusive, and somehow not spoiling the view of the tranquillity.

It was a perfect place, an ideal home for a warrior who'd given up fighting the quiet battles of his profession. Aura stood for long moments, until the sound of a car coming down the road froze her into place.

Please don't let it be Flint, she prayed.

She stood with her face turned away and unease crystallising into panic in her stomach as the car slowed, then stopped.

A voice with a distinct French intonation said, 'You are lost, *m'selle*?'

Slowly, reluctantly, Aura turned. There was only one person in the car. Relief sent colour licking through her cheeks. 'No, I'm just admiring the view.'

It was the Frenchman Flint was in partnership with. Although he was eyeing her with typical Gallic appreciation, she found nothing offensive in his candid admiration.

'Me, also, I am admiring the view,' he said with a twinkle, and she laughed.

The breeze caught her scarf. She managed to catch it before it tore free from her hair, but he said nevertheless, 'It is a crime to hide such hair.'

She smiled, and said, 'The wind's a little busy. Goodbye, *monsieur*.'

She liked him, she thought as she drove home. She could be very happy there, beside the river, with the vines growing about her. She liked Warkworth, too.

Oh, who was she fooling? If Flint asked her she would live with him on the top of Mt Cook, the highest mountain in New Zealand, called by the Maori people Aoraki, the cloud piercer.

That night she cried a little before she went to sleep, but somehow the visit had eased a sore patch in her heart.

The next day she caught a plane to Fala'isi for another shoot.

Fala'isi was an island in the Pacific, set like a green jewel in a sea so blue it hurt the eyes. The crew was booked in for the usual hectic week, and on the last evening just before dinner Aura was disturbed by a telephone call from New Zealand.

'Aura?' It was Jessica, her voice tinny and far away.

'Jess? What's the matter?' The telephone seemed to have waves on the line, a positive sea of them, and behind the crackle and hiss Jessica's voice ebbed and flowed, so that all she could hear were disconnected words.

'—asked where—didn't, of course—but—so I wanted to make sure——'

'Jess, I can't hear more than a word you're saying! There must be sunspots, or something. Look, fax would be better.'

'What?'

'Fax it. F-A-X.'

'Oh, all right. No, wait——' Inexorably her voice faded into static.

Aura sighed, fossicked through the information the hotel had packaged for visitors, found the fax number and read it out, slowly and clearly, three times.

'OK,' Jessica said clearly before another wave of electronic interference broke over the line.

Aura put the telephone down and rubbed gently between her brows, telling herself very firmly not to frown. It hadn't worried her before, she had felt free to do what she wanted with her face, but modelling tended to make you conscious of such things. In many ways it was a narcissistic way to earn a living. She admired the creativity that went into it and the models for their sheer stamina, and she would always be grateful for the money she earned, but she would be glad to give it up.

Picking up a towel, she went off down to the beach.

She expected to find a fax waiting for her when she came back, but enquiries revealed that nothing had arrived. Probably Jessica had decided it wasn't worth worrying about, she thought with resignation. After all, she'd be in Auckland in thirty-six hours.

She ate dinner with the rest of the crew, turned down an invitation to an island night, and went up to bed. It had been three months now, and she shouldn't still be missing Flint with every breath of her body, every heart beat, as though someone had torn a necessary part of her away.

Perhaps it was just because she was back in the tropics. Not that Fala'isi was much like Australia, beyond the superficial resemblance of heat and palms and a warm sea. The sound of this sea resounded in her ears, its great smooth rollers crashing on to the reef that protected the white beaches, and the air smelt faintly of the tang of the tropics, coconut and sweetly scented flowers and salt, the rich, moist scent of fertility and life.

She switched off her light and lay on her side, looking at the window. If only Flint hadn't been so remote that last morning. She had known then that it was over. If they had quarrelled she could have used the emotion to connect with him, but she had no weapons against that calm, impersonal kindness, that armour of self-possession.

A tear gathered in the corner of her eye, trickled on to her pillow. But she would not cry. There must be an end to this pain sooner or later.

The rest of the crew left on the early morning plane, but, as she'd decided to stay on a day, she planned to lie late in bed. However, dawn found her awake, so she got up and put on shorts and a top and went down through the quiet hotel, exchanging greetings with the few people who were about, then walked along the gleaming sand, looking at the small island on the reef where she had been photographed the day before.

A tall figure at the far end of the beach made her grimace; she didn't want to have to smile at anyone else. She would turn before he did, and head off along the other way. In the meantime she ordered herself to enjoy the freshness of the air, already warm, yet tangy with the scent of the forest on the high inland mountains, and the soft sound of the waves as they touched languidly on to the coarse white coral sand. The sun caught spray as a particularly large comber hit the reef, and for a second rainbows hung suspended in the crystal air.

Sudden tears prolonged the rainbow. Aura sniffed. Here it was always summer. At home, in spite of the show of freesias with their exquisite lemon scent, and daphne, spicy and pink, it was still spring, and the year was just gearing up for the magical slow slide into summer.

Homesickness washed over her. It had been a mistake to stay the extra day. If she had left with the crew she would have been in Auckland by now. She turned abruptly and walked as quickly as she could down the beach and into the hotel.

A touch on her shoulder made her jump and whirl around.

'Why are you crying?' Flint asked curtly as she stared at him in something very close to horror.

'Was that you on the beach?' she said stupidly.

He nodded. He looked the same, impregnable as ever, and she hated him for it. She'd been slowly dying inside, and he'd just gone on his way without feeling anything. No doubt when he thought of her it was with a faint contempt. Or did he think she was a good one-night stand?

Because whatever other opinion he had of her, he couldn't deny that. It had been as good for him as it was for her.

It was ironically amusing, when you thought of it. She had given her virginity to a man who thought she was little better than a whore.

And she had the feeling that she was never going to be able to find another man to live up to him.

CHAPTER EIGHT

'WHAT are you doing here?' Aura asked jerkily, averting her face. 'Or is this just a coincidence, like the last time you found me in a hotel?'

'No.' Flint spoke with a clipped intonation that made her withdraw even further. 'This time I came looking for you.'

'How did you know where I was?' she croaked, voicing the first foolish question that came to mind because she couldn't ask the more important ones.

'I rang Jessica. She told me.'

'No. She wouldn't tell anyone where I was.' Of course, that's what last night's call had been about. Jessica had been trying to warn her.

He smiled unpleasantly. 'Oh, when I told her why I wanted to see you she gave me your address.'

'Why?' she asked warily.

'Why did I hunt you down?' He put his hand into the pocket of his trousers and pulled out a river of green fire. 'To return these.'

Aura's eyes widened, but she made no attempt to take them from him. 'Where did you find those?' she demanded. The day after she had signed the contract she had gone to the jeweller's to buy them back, but they had already been resold.

'I bought them.'

She swallowed. 'Why?'

His smile was self-derisory. 'Oh, put it down to sentimentality.'

Frowning, she asked, 'How did you know I'd sold them?'

'I met your cousin Alick one day in Auckland. He'd just come empty-handed out of the jeweller's. Apparently Natalie had gone weeping to him to ask him if he could buy them back.'

Her face lit up. 'Dear Alick,' she said tenderly.

He slid the chain of green fire through his fingers, watching them with narrowed eyes. 'Unfortunately, dear Alick was unsuccessful, and he had to leave for Frankfurt the next day. The jeweller couldn't tell him who had bought them—they'd been through a couple of hands since he sold them, gaining value as they went—but he did say he'd heard a rumour that they were going to America.'

'So how did they get here?' Aura asked tentatively.

He looked into her face. 'I offered to track them down, which I did. Then I made the buyer an offer he couldn't refuse.'

'For Alick?'

'No,' he said, smiling unpleasantly, 'for me.'

'But why?' she asked numbly.

He laughed softly. 'I said it was for sentimental reasons. You wore them the night I first kissed you, remember? The night at the opera. I've always hoped that one night I'll make love to you when you're wearing nothing but your lovely skin and these.'

He tossed the necklace towards her. It sparkled and flashed in the drowsy air. Aura caught it, feeling the weight and the interplay of colours, the cool smoothness of the gold warmed by his body heat.

'Why did you bring them here?' she whispered.

He hesitated, then said, 'Because you came up to Matakana.'

She closed her eyes. Had he been there, watching her? Humiliation clogged her throat, cast a clammy pall over her skin. 'How do you know?'

'Jean-Pierre told me.'

'He doesn't know me.'

Flint's mouth moved in a cold smile. 'No, but when he raved about a woman with hair the colour of the best burgundy, and great green eyes that were sad enough to kill oneself for, and a mouth that was made to speak French, not clumsy English, I knew who he'd seen.'

Aura said nothing; she was too busy cursing herself for giving in to that compelling need to see the vineyard.

Flint said, 'We can't talk here. Come up to my suite.'

He spoke so matter-of-factly that she couldn't find the words to object, and within minutes she found herself in an opulent sitting-room, so many questions fighting for supremacy that she couldn't ask any of them.

She stood irresolutely, watching his reflection in the mirror as he picked up a telephone and ordered breakfast from room-service. Broad shoulders and lean hips, an effortless animal grace that sent shivers of response down her body; the arrogant epitome of force and power.

When he had replaced the receiver he turned to where she hovered beside a leather sofa and commanded, 'Sit down. I'm not going to eat you.'

Not yet, anyway, his smile and glance, swift and predatory, promised.

Aura sat down, and this time she was able to ask, 'Why did you go to so much trouble?'

'Can't you guess, Aura?'

Slowly she shook her head. 'No.'

'What have you been doing since I saw you last?'

'Working.'

'Still modelling?'

Her hackles rose at the distaste in his voice, but she said firmly and without emotion, 'Yes.'

'Why did you take it up?' He spoke idly, but she knew him too well. There was nothing idle in his interest.

She shrugged. 'You know why. For the same reason I sold the garnets. I needed the money.'

'Your mother's just married an extremely rich man. By all accounts he's as generous as he is rich, and he's certainly besotted by Natalie. You don't have to work. You could have an idyllic life with them.'

Still not looking at him she said coolly, 'No.' She would never take money from a man.

His dark brows lifted, but he pursued, 'You're doing fairly well, I gather. Do you plan to make it your career?'

'No. At the beginning of next year I'm looking for a job.'

For some reason this amused him. 'Really? What?'

'I did a double major in information systems and marketing,' she said acidly. 'I don't expect to have much difficulty finding work.'

This time she surprised him. His brows shot up further and he looked more than a little taken aback. 'I see.'

Something compelled her to add, 'Didn't Paul tell you?'

'Paul and I didn't discuss you at all,' he said shortly.

She raised delicately mocking brows. 'How about this dossier you had compiled?'

His smile was ironic. 'It was sketchy, little more than gossip. I told you about it to gauge your reaction. I'm afraid I imagined your degree to be the usual fashionable BA. Paul may have tried to tell me, but I cut him off whenever he started to talk about you. Where did you do this degree?'

It couldn't do any harm to tell him. 'At a polytech in West Auckland.'

'What decided you to graduate in those subjects?' he asked absently.

She shot him a suspicious look, but there was nothing to be discerned in the harsh features but mild interest. 'Originally I decided to be an accountant.' Her mouth twisted wryly. 'It seemed a good idea, and maths and accounting were two of my best subjects at school.'

A quiet knock on the door heralded a waiter with a breakfast trolley. When he had finished setting the table and was gone, Flint said, 'Would you like to pour the coffee?'

He didn't tell her how he had it and she didn't ask. She had forgotten nothing about him. Although the food smelt divine as only coffee and bacon could, he didn't sit down. Nor did he ask her more about her education.

Instead he said distantly, 'Have you seen Paul lately?'

Aura flinched. 'No.'

'Neither have I, but I hear he's recovering.'

'Good. I'm glad.'

He walked across to a window, stopping to stare moodily out at the sunny beach. Someone was sweeping the sand, singing in a deep bass one of the cheerful songs that seemed to grow in the very air here.

Aura sipped a little coffee, then put the cup back. She looked at the food, but her hunger had died.

'That's not why I wanted to see you,' he said at last. 'Why did you go up to Matakana?'

Aura's heart began to beat heavily in her breast, in the hollow at the base of her throat, echoing in her ears. She looked down at her coffee, noting the way the steam wisped across the rich liquid in the bone-china cup.

'I read an article in a magazine,' she admitted reluctantly. 'I just wanted to see the place.'

'Did you like it?'

'Oh, yes. It was beautiful.'

Another silence.

Then, 'I tracked you down,' he said deliberately, 'because I've discovered that I can't live without you.'

Coffee cascaded into her saucer. Aura managed to straighten it before any overflowed further, but her hands were trembling too much to hold it safely, so she had to set cup and saucer down on the table with a little chink that sounded far too loud in the quiet room. She sat with her head bowed, unable to look away, her whole attention bent on the words that had just rasped past her ear.

'Did you hear me?' he demanded.

'Yes, I heard you.' Her voice was cool and steady.

'And,' he said deliberately, 'because it seemed that if you'd taken the trouble to come up to Matakana you were at least getting over Paul.'

'It's a matter of having to,' she said stonily.

'Do you still dream about him?'

She shook her head. Still not looking at him she said, 'It was only that once. Flint, it won't work.'

'Why not?'

'Because I don't——'

'I know that I've done everything possible to make you hate me, but there were times when you liked me, Aura. When we aren't fighting we get on well. And now there's no reason to fight.' His urgent interruption caught her attention as nothing else could.

She looked up. He had turned his head and was watching her. The autocratic pirate's face was set in lines of rigid control.

'Flint...' she began, exhausted.

With the speed of a cornered animal, he came away from the window. Before Aura had a chance to continue he pulled her up from the sofa and into his arms, holding her tightly against the disciplined male hardness of his body.

'If there's no other way,' he said in a voice that ached through her, a voice where cynicism and a black desire were blended, 'I can reach you like this.'

His mouth crushed her protests, reduced them to cyphers in her brain, to shadows, and then to oblivion. The kiss had something of desperation in it, as though he had been starved for this, had lain awake for long nights eaten by need for her.

For a second Aura resisted, until a reciprocal fire and passion overwhelmed her self-control. Her endless yearning and the sudden masculine assault swept away her defences. She sank into mindlessness, glorying in capitulation, dimly aware in some distant region of her brain that her surrender was composed of intricate strands of conquest and yielding woven together to form a pattern of equality.

Eventually he lifted his mouth to mutter, 'If this is all there is for you, it will do for the time being. You drive me mad, you've taken up residence in my heart, in my mind, in my soul, and nothing I can do will get rid of you. I've never needed a woman before, never wanted one that I couldn't do without, but you stormed into my heart, demolished all the walls and took it over, and since the first time I saw you I've been only half a person.'

Aura said with difficulty, 'It's not——'

'No,' he said. 'Don't say no, not yet. Let me dream a little longer.'

'Flint——' The rest of the sentence was obliterated by another kiss. Sighing, Aura gave herself up to rapture, returning it with all the passion that was in her.

'You do want me,' he said at last when she was breathless and trembling, looking at her with such naked passion blazing in his golden eyes that her resistance leached away.

She smiled sadly. 'Of course I want you.'

His smile was a mixture of triumph and pain. 'I don't know how to deal with this. I thought it would be easy, that I'd use this violent attraction between us to get you into my bed, and then infiltrate your defences so cunningly that before you knew it you'd love me. But I'm greedy; I want it all, and I want it now.'

'What do you want?' He didn't answer, merely watched her with intent, half-closed eyes. 'What do you want?' she insisted.

He looked away, his face hard and taut and hungry. 'I suppose you deserve your pound of flesh.'

Releasing her, he stepped back. After a momentary hesitation he said through his teeth, 'I want you to love me as much as I love you.'

Aura's heart went into overdrive. '*Do* you love me?' she asked, dry-mouthed.

'Of course I bloody well love you!' He stared furiously at her, and then laughed, a harsh, mirthless sound. 'If you knew how many times I've tried to work out how I'd approach you. I thought, she deserves tenderness, she's had precious little of it, so I'll be tender. But I can't do it, not without knowing how you feel.'

'All you had to say,' she said quietly, 'was that you loved me. Because I've loved you since the second time we met.'

He went white, then as the dark colour flooded back into his skin he grabbed her in a swift, clumsily desperate movement that was a far cry from his usual grace. He didn't kiss her again; for long seconds he stood staring over her head, with his arms so tight around her that she could barely breathe, his heart beating like a triphammer against her.

He swore, muttering something short and succinct and vicious. And then at last his arms loosened, and he pushed her chin up, gazing into her eyes. Aura looked back, her mouth curving.

'That bloody smile,' he said quietly. 'You looked at me like that that first night, and I thought—oh, God, I thought, what the hell am I going to do about this? All right, you little witch. When are you going to marry me?'

Her heart leapt into her throat, and then the light died in her eyes and he demanded, 'What is it?'

'We can't get married,' she said miserably.

'Why not?'

'Paul——'

His arms slackened a moment, and she tried to step away, but he said angrily, 'No. He's not going to stand between us like an angel with a flaming sword, I'm damned if he is.'

'But he's your friend.'

'And you,' he said smoothly, 'are going to be my wife.'

'He'll hate it,' she said, giving in, not realising it.

Her words fell like heavy stones into mud, flat, no reverberation, no echo.

'Yes,' he replied uncompromisingly, 'I'm afraid he will. But there is nothing we can do about that. We are not responsible for Paul's happiness.'

She bit her lip. 'I didn't want to come between you.'

'There's nothing for you to come between. He doesn't consider me a friend any longer. And even if he did, I'm not going to wait for years until he's got over you. These last few months have been hell, waiting for you to get him out of your system. Aura, I love you, and I'm damned sure you love me. Our commitment has to be to each other. I want us to marry.'

Against that simple statement of need she had no defences. 'Yes,' she said simply. 'All right.'

He stood very still. 'Just like that?' he asked incredulously.

Her smile quivered on her lips. 'What do you expect me to do? Object for the sake of objection? You know I love you.'

'I thought you might have some mistaken loyalty that would keep you away from me.' He laughed softly, exultantly, and kissed her forehead. 'I thought I might have to take you to bed again and again until I got you pregnant, and then persuade you into marrying me. Actually, I was rather looking forward to that.'

She laughed too, her green eyes tender and soft and amused. 'I'll bet,' she said. 'I can see I'm going to have a hell of a life.'

His arms were warm and strong about her, offering not safety but risk, not tranquillity but excitement, nothing of the kind tenderness she had thought she wanted. Flint was fire and danger and exhilarating turbulence; life with him would be far removed from the haven of serene calm she had longed for. And she wouldn't have it any other way.

Smiling, she lifted her face in mute invitation.

Hours later, when the swift tropical darkness had enveloped the island in its purple embrace, she stirred. Instantly Flint's arms tightened around her.

'No,' he said into her ear.

Smiling, she rubbed her cheek against the swell of his chest. 'I'm not going anywhere.'

'Good.' He yawned, then kissed the tangle of hair that swirled across his shoulder. 'Each time we make love I think nothing could be better, nothing could ever match it again, and each time it's more exciting, more unbearably electrifying. I suppose one day I'll get so excited I'll die.'

'Not while we're making love, I hope,' she said, laughing.

He grinned, the lazy, eminently satisfied smile of a man who has the world in his grasp. There was something very tigerish in that smile. 'Why not? It would be a wonderful way to go.'

'For you, perhaps. I wouldn't like it at all.'

'OK, I won't.' His arms contracted about her. 'When are you going to marry me?'

'I've got a photo shoot in Thailand in a fortnight's time, and a trip to Japan in January. I can't get out of them, Flint.'

For some reason she expected him to object, but he said calmly, 'No, there's no reason why you should even try. Shall we get married before you go to Thailand?'

'So soon?'

He laughed at her scandalised tone, his golden eyes gleaming with tender mockery. 'Why not? Do you want a big wedding?'

'No!'

His shoulders moved in a shrug. 'So why wait? I have to work for Robertson's until the end of the year, and then we can move to the vineyard. We'll need to build a couple of houses; I'd contracted the same architect who designed the winery, but as soon as I realised I was in love with you I put him off; you're going to have to approve his plans. Jean-Pierre is very magnanimous; he says he'll stay in his caravan until our house is finished, provided you cook him a couple of dinners a week. You'll like him.'

Aura looked down into his confident, hard-hewn face. People didn't change just because they were in love. Natalie was still Natalie, and Flint would always try to bulldoze her into doing what he wanted.

'What if I can't cook?' she asked demurely.

'He'll teach you,' he said, laughter tilting the corners of his mouth.

'As it happens, I'm not a bad cook, but I'm always ready to take lessons. If you put the architect on hold you must have been pretty confident I'd marry you.' Her voice was very wry.

He grinned. 'It was the only way I could stop myself from slitting my wrists.' The humour leached from his face. 'I had to believe you'd get over Paul and turn to me, otherwise I think I'd have gone mad. For the first time in my life I was desperate.'

'I'll bet you were hell to live with.'

He flushed slightly, and laughed again. 'You know me too well,' he said drily. 'Well, will you be happy living on a vineyard?'

'It sounds wonderful.'

He kissed her soft mouth. 'Of course. Everything's wonderful. In fact, if I'd tried we couldn't have worked things better. The business is going to need a good accountant and money manager, and you are clearly sent by providence to be that.'

She pulled a face. 'You don't even know yet whether I can do it.'

'Am I taking too much for granted? Would you rather work in town?'

For the first time Aura allowed herself to hope that this time everything would work out, that the future would be as bright and shining as it seemed to promise. She said, 'What would you do if I said I would?'

His hand in her hair contracted, but he said evenly, 'I'll try to persuade you that you'd be happier working with me, but I'm not an ogre, my heart, my darling. You will make your own life.'

'I can't think of anything I'd like more than working with you.'

He kissed her, and kissed her again, and after a highly satisfactory interval she sighed, and asked the question that had been nagging at her ever since the last time they'd been together.

'Why did you make love to me that first time? Not that first time we——' beneath his amused glance colour heated her skin, but she kept on doggedly '—we—ah—slept together, but in Auckland. After *The Pearl Fishers*.'

He was silent for a moment. Then he said heavily, 'I was desperate to stop you from marrying Paul, driven by a compulsion stronger than honour or friendship. At the time it seemed all I could do was bypass your better self and home in on the sexual attraction, because I knew you felt that just as strongly as I did. It was the only way to break the ties of loyalty that bound you to him. But as well, I couldn't resist. You had me so tied up in knots that I had to kiss you. Perhaps I even thought that it might do nothing for me, that it was only because you were forbidden that I wanted you.'

She flinched, and he said harshly, 'Yes,' and in the monosyllable was all his pain and self-disgust, and beneath it, like true metal under corrosion, the shining edifice of his love. 'But if I did,' he went on, 'that first kiss showed me just how wrong I was. I knew then that I had to have you. Yet although your response nearly blew my mind, you were still determined to marry him.'

She said, 'I loved him. But after that night I knew I couldn't marry him.'

'You knew?' Lifting her chin, he stared down into her face with quick antagonism. 'Then why the hell didn't you tell me?'

'How could I? Not before I told him—I owed him that, at least. I had to wait until he came back from Samoa. And I didn't know how you felt. You told me you weren't offering anything but an affair. I was utterly wretched.'

'You and me both.' The anger died as fast as it came; he kissed her gently, stroking her hair away from her cheek. 'I needed you to want me because you loved me, not for security, not for any other reason but that you couldn't live without me. When you still wouldn't give in, I realised I'd have to force the issue. I know Paul. Under that surface placidness there's a very possessive man. He'd have tried to keep you any way he could.'

'He didn't,' she said.

'Because I told him we were already lovers.'

She sat up and stared at him. 'You *what*?'

In spite of her indignant struggles he tucked her back against him. 'Calm down. It was the only thing I could think of to keep him away from you, and even then I didn't know whether it would work.'

'You lied,' she said dangerously.

'Yes. Don't worry, it's not a habit. I won't lie to you ever, I swear. I was damned near in despair. You see, I always knew you loved him. That's why I asked you not to see him by yourself, when I got called away. I thought he might be able to persuade you to go ahead with the wedding. If you had, you'd have torn yourself and him to pieces. Because I would have taken you away from him. You and I were meant to be, my darling.'

He had understood much more than she gave him credit for. She lay for a long time with her cheek against the steady throb of his heart.

At last he said unevenly, 'God, I could have ripped up the whole world when that bloody beeper sounded, but there was nothing I could do, nothing I could think of in the way of damage control except to ask you to stay away from him.'

'And you left me in Cairns because you thought I was still in love with him?'

He kissed the top of her head, his arms tightening around her. 'You were still bound to him, emotionally if not legally. You needed time.'

She nodded. Flint had the clearer vision. She had been anchored to the past by chains of memory, and they had been flawed and false. She didn't want peace and tranquillity, a husband who worshipped her as though she was something rare and fragile to be kept safe, locked away from harm. She needed a challenge, just as he did; Flint understood her better than she did herself.

Soberly she said, 'Yes. I did love him. But I love you far more, and I'm in love with you as well. I know the difference now. I think perhaps I always did; I just wasn't ready to admit it.' She told him about the dream she had had the night she had met him. 'I should have listened to what it was trying to tell me,' she finished.

'You wouldn't be the woman I love if you'd just dumped him. I knew you had to have time to get over him,' he said sombrely. 'At Cairns I was starving and afraid. I used the attraction between us to get you into bed—and found to my delight that it was the first time for you—but I couldn't go on doing that. You had to put him into the past where he belonged, and learn to love me, and to do that you had to have time, without pressure, time to discover the truth for yourself.'

She turned her hot face into his neck. 'How did you know that it was the first time?'

'Oh, it was all very new to you.' His smile was wickedly satisfied. 'It wasn't difficult to realise why. I know it's not modern to say that I'm glad you were a virgin, but I felt like the ruler of the universe when I realised.'

'Chauvinist,' she accused.

'In this, I'm afraid so. Unrepentant, too. Saying goodbye to you that morning was the hardest thing I've ever done, but too much had happened too fast. I told myself I'd wait patiently for some sign from you.' He laughed. 'Although I must admit I was getting damned restless when Jean-Pierre told me you'd come up to the vineyard.'

'Mm.' She kissed his jaw, and along the scar, her eyes dreamy. 'I do love you,' she said.

'And I love you. With all my heart.'

EPILOGUE

'AURA, what the hell are you doing in there?' Beneath the exasperation in Flint's tone was the ever-present note of tenderness, discernible even through the dressing-room door.

Aura grinned. 'I'm getting dressed.'

'It had better be worth this wait.'

'Trust me,' she growled seductively.

'I don't trust you an inch, but I'll wait another five minutes.'

Pulling a face at the door, she slid pearls into her ears, one creamy white, one black, two teardrops that must have cost Flint a fortune three years ago when their son was born.

'There,' she told her reflection, 'you're ready. And though I say so myself, you look stunning.'

The freshly floral scent of Joy floated up to her nostrils as she opened the door and walked into the bedroom, sleek and sophisticated in a wool georgette dress the exact colour of her skin. Its narrow skirt revealed legs in the sheerest of stockings and high plain, ivory shoes. Seen from the front the dress was demure, with loose long sleeves and soft folds, but at the back the material was draped in a deep cowl that showed her spine almost to her waist. A wide satin band hugged her hips, finishing with a bow at one side.

She had put her hair up and clipped a matching satin bow at the back of her head. It was definitely dressing to kill, and from the look on Flint's face when he saw her she had succeeded.

181

'There,' she said, twirling so that he could see the back. Smiling, she looked over her shoulder. 'Was it worth waiting for?'

'You're always worth waiting for,' he said, examining her with the bold eye of possession. 'But this time you've outdone yourself. How long do we have to stay at this thing?'

Laughing, she finished her twirl, stopping just in front of him so that she could look up into his fierce face. 'Until, my darling, everyone at this presentation has decided that Southern Red is the most exciting development in wine-making that's hit the world since the Californian experience.'

He sighed elaborately, spanning her waist with hands that were strong and lean and tanned with years of working in the vineyard. 'It is,' he said, his voice ringing with confidence. 'It's going to be right up there with the best in ten years' time.'

'I know.'

He laughed under his breath. 'You never doubted, did you? Not even when people told us we were crazy.'

She shook her head. 'No. You once told me that you were not in the habit of making mistakes. I believe you.'

'I was damned arrogant.' His hands tightened for a moment and the golden glitter of his glance sharpened. 'It's a wonder you let me anywhere near you.'

Aura reached up and cupped his cheek. 'You're still arrogant,' she said pertly. 'But I love you.'

His grin was part teasing, part amusement, all pure male satisfaction. 'You know, I must have had all the gods on my side when I fell in love with you. You've worked wonders. Thanks to you we've come in well under budget, and the publicity has been tremendous. Who but you would have decided to launch our first vintage with a reception in a marquee? Silk-lined, at that? And managed to whip up such a storm of publicity that we've even had British wine buyers asking for invitations?'

She hugged him. 'They wanted to come because the wine is magnificent,' she said. 'And that, my dear heart, is because you and Jean-Pierre are brilliant. Everyone senses history in the making. And it's going to get better. Darling, this is the start of a dynasty! Now, we'd better go. I'm sure your mother thinks no one can cook crayfish as well as she does. I've already had to haul her out of the kitchen twice. She just doesn't seem to understand that she's here to be fussed over and waited on.'

'Not my mother,' Flint said cheerfully.

Aura laughed. The house was full, with Natalie and Joe occupying one bedroom, and Flint's parents in another. They had very little in common, yet they seemed to get on like a house on fire.

Life, she thought, as she turned down the stairs, had very little more it could offer her.

'Hello, Aura.'

For a painful second she froze, before slowly turning. Yes, it was Paul, five years older, his blue eyes watchful beneath hooded lids.

'Paul,' she said, and her smile broke through. 'Paul, how wonderful to see you!'

'Ah, it's great to see you, too. Marriage and motherhood and growing wine obviously agrees with you.'

'It does, indeed. You look good, too. Have you talked to Flint?'

'I've seen him. I haven't spoken to him. I'm a bit embarrassed—the last time we met I said some totally unforgivable things to him.'

Flint had never spoken of that final interview, but since then neither man had seen the other, and she knew that the loss of Paul's friendship still hurt her husband.

'He forgives a lot more easily than he used to,' she said drily.

'There were things I had no right to say,' Paul said, looking at her intently. 'I'm afraid I blamed him for——'

'It doesn't matter.'

'I've missed you both.'

'Then why don't you go and say something to him, Paul?'

He nodded. 'Yes, I think I will. You're even more beautiful than I remember. I hear you have children.'

'A son, Andrew Paul,' she said deliberately, 'and a daughter, Sophie. Andrew's three now, and Sophie is eighteen months. How about you, Paul? Are you married?'

'No,' he said, smiling faintly. 'Perhaps I had to exorcise you.'

Aura laughed. 'And now you have.'

'And now I have,' he said slowly, and laughed too. 'I think I knew even when we got engaged that you weren't in love with me, although you loved me. It was pride and bloody-mindedness that made me so obstinate.'

'You're too hard on yourself.'

'I'm not a fast learner, but eventually I get there,' he said, but absently, and with his eyes fixed above Aura's head on someone approaching.

The familiar sizzle in her nerves warned Aura of Flint's arrival. She turned her head and smiled, letting him see that she wasn't in the least worried by the encounter. Something dangerous in the golden eyes faded.

He looked across at the man who had once been his best friend. 'Paul,' he said, his voice giving nothing away.

Paul's smile was twisted but he held out his hand. 'It's good to see you, Flint,' he said, and there was no mistaking the sincerity in his voice.

They shook hands, and Aura relaxed. It was going to be all right.

Much later that night, when everyone had gone and they were back in their bedroom overlooking the silent river and the Sandspit and their glimpse of Kawau Island across the bay, she said demurely, 'Well, I think that was a success, don't you?'

He laughed, and kissed the back of her neck. 'Don't fish. It was a magnificent success, and you were perfect. Darling, you tied my life up with a big ribbon when you married me.'

'Well, at least no one is going to forget Southern Red in a hurry,' she said, smiling at their reflections in the mirror.

'Oh, we're properly on the map. And next year the vintage is going to be even better. I like your idea of founding a dynasty. How many children does it take to found one?'

'Well, Andy tells me he's going to be a grader driver, so we'll have to do without him. I think we should budget for a couple of extras,' she said soberly, 'just in case Sophie decides not to become a winegrower.'

He flung his head back and laughed, his strong arms hugging her against him. Aura's eyes glimmered greenly beneath half-closed lids. They had such a good life, she and her love; she had never known that happiness could swell up inside you and colour the world.

She turned and kissed him, then slid free. 'Do you think you and Paul will ever be real friends again?'

'I hope so.' He dropped cufflinks on to the dressing-table.

'I'm glad he came,' she said, sliding the pearls from her ears and putting them carefully away in their box. 'He's been on my conscience.'

'Mine, too.' His eyes gleamed, little flames licking up through their translucence, setting fire to every cell in her body. 'Did I tell you that wherever you walked to-night people stopped talking and watched you? And every man's face had the same look—awe and envy.'

'You might have muttered something like that,' she said, smiling, 'but you can always tell me again. Not that I care about any other man but you.'

'I know. And I can't tell you how that makes me feel,' he said. 'Like the luckiest man in the world.'

Her eyes misted. 'You got more than your share of looks,' she said. 'Women go all wobbly and weak-kneed when you smile that tiger's smile at them. And I distinctly heard Jess groan when you kissed her.'

'Sam should take her in hand,' he said, but absently. 'You know, I've spent all evening wondering about that dress. Hold out your hand.'

She did so, and he slowly began to undo the little buttons at her wrist. While his deft fingers moved across the pale material he told her what he planned to do when he had taken the exquisite thing from her, his words explicit yet tender, so that when at last he pulled it over her head and she was standing there in silk briefs and stockings and her shoes, she was blushing all over.

'If Paul had never spoken to me for the rest of my life,' he said, eyes glittering like jewels, 'it would be worth it. You are my world now, you and the children. You're all that's worthwhile to me, all that I need, all that I hope for. I go to bed at night with you in my mind, and when I wake I think of you. I've never regretted what happened.'

She slid into his arms, hugging him fiercely, feeling the increasing speed of his heart, the little signs that revealed to her just how she was affecting him.

'Neither have I,' she said quietly. 'It took me a long time to accept that if we hadn't met before I married Paul it would have made no difference. Married or not, I love you, and I would have followed you without a backward glance. That's what made me feel so guilty.'

'Yes.' He looked down at her face, his own hard and predatory. 'Me, too. I'd have broken Paul's marriage as easily as I broke his engagement. Without a qualm, throwing away a lifetime's friendship, because you were *my* woman, not his.' His voice roughened into a harsh purr. He bent and kissed the pulse that throbbed in the base of her throat. 'Because I love you,' he said against her skin. 'Because you are my other half.'

'Because we were meant for each other.'

He lifted her and carried her across to the bed, his face intent and purposeful, the dark fires of his love no longer threatening. As Aura drew him down to her, scanning his beloved face with slumbrous eyes, she smiled.

Harlequin invites you to the most
romantic wedding of the season.

Rope the cowboy of your dreams in
Marry Me, Cowboy!

A collection of 4 brand-new stories,
celebrating weddings, written by:

New York Times bestselling author

JANET DAILEY

and favorite authors

Margaret Way
Anne McAllister
Susan Fox

Be sure not to miss Marry Me, Cowboy!
coming this April

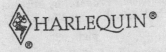

PRESENTS
RELUCTANT BRIDEGROOMS

Two beautiful brides, two unforgettable romances…
two men running for their lives.…

My Lady Love, by Paula Marshall, introduces
Charles, Viscount Halstead, who lost his memory
and found himself employed as a stableboy by the
untouchable Nell Tallboys, Countess Malplaquet.
But Nell didn't consider Charles untouchable—
not at all!

Darling Amazon, by Sylvia Andrew, is the story of
a spurious engagement between Julia Marchant
and Hugo, marquess of Rostherne—an engagement
that gets out of hand and just may lead Hugo to
the altar after all!

Enjoy two madcap Regency weddings this May,
wherever Harlequin books are sold.